DISCARD
W9-BXM-066
TWEEN FICTION B

THE CASE THAT TIME FORGOT

TRACY BARRETT

Henry Holt and Company
New York

Henry Holt and Company, LLC
Publishers since 1866
175 Fifth Avenue
New York, New York 10010
www.HenryHoltKids.com

Distributed in Canada by H. B. Fenn and Company Ltd.

Library of Congress Cataloging-in-Publication Data
Barrett, Tracy.
The case that time forgot / by Tracy Barrett. — 1st ed.
p. cm. — (The Sherlock files ; 3)
Summary: Xena and Xander Holmes, an American brother and sister who are living in England, use clues from their ancestor Sherlock Holmes's casebook when they are asked by a classmate to find an ancient Egyptian artifact that has been missing for many years.
ISBN 978-0-8050-8046-9
[1. Mystery and detective stories. 2. Brothers and sisters—Fiction. 3. Egypt—Antiquities—Fiction. 4. London (England)—Fiction. 5. England—Fiction.] I. Title.
PZ7.B275355Cas 2010 [Fic]—dc22 2009024148

First Edition—2010 / Book designed by Greg Wozney
Printed in March 2010 in the United States of America
by R. R. Donnelley & Sons Company, Harrisonburg, Virginia

10 9 8 7 6 5 4 3 2 1

CHAPTER ONE

At first, Xander Holmes thought that the slip of paper must have fallen out of his own notebook. But even as he stooped to pick it up, he noticed some details that most people wouldn't have seen. This was partly genetic—he was, after all, the great-great-great grandson of the famous detective Sherlock Holmes—and partly habit. He and his sister, Xena, had started solving mysteries several months earlier, shortly after their arrival in London.

The paper was normal notebook paper, white with faint blue lines. It had been folded and refolded into a narrow rectangle. The size of the slit in my locker, Xander thought, and then, I don't remember folding any paper like that.

He paused. What else? The ink used by whoever had written on it had bled through a bit. His pens didn't do that.

It was probably just a note from his sister or

one of his friends. The lockers at school had been installed only recently, while the students were on fall break, and he wasn't used to them yet. Probably people left notes in lockers all the time. He unfolded the paper.

He was still staring at the writing and trying to figure out what it meant when the locker next to his slammed shut. He looked up to see red-headed Andrew Watson, a friend and fellow member of the SPFD, the Society for the Preservation of Famous Detectives.

"What a pain these lockers are," Andrew grumbled. "You should figure out who's been stealing things so we can go back to storing our gear in our desks like before."

Xander understood that Andrew was just being grouchy, as usual. Andrew knew that he and Xena only investigated problems from Sherlock Holmes's notebook of unsolved cases. The SPFD had given them the precious casebook, and Xander and Xena had already solved two of its most baffling cases.

"Did you hear that Jill Fenton had her MP3 player nicked this morning?" Andrew asked.

"Uh, no," Xander said. He wasn't really paying attention. He was too intrigued by what he was looking at to think about anything else.

What the paper said was odd enough, but it was the handwriting that interested him. Did anybody write like that, for real? It was all in capitals, and was written so plainly that it looked like a page from a penmanship book for little kids.

"Xander!" His sister was coming down the hall toward him. She was chatting with Hannah, her new friend. Xena's long dark hair with its blond streak looked almost black next to Hannah's light brown curls. She was followed by two boys named Shane and Jake. They played on what Xander still thought of as the varsity soccer team, despite the fact that they didn't say "varsity" in England. Xander, two years younger, was on what would be the junior varsity in the States.

Xena came up to Xander while the others stopped to talk with Andrew.

"What are you *doing*?" she asked. "I called you three times. I wanted to tell you I'm staying late after school with Hannah. I phoned Mom to say I'll come home with you after your soccer practice." She paused. "What's so fascinating about that paper?"

He handed it to her. "It's weird. I can't figure out what it is."

Xena read the few lines on the paper:

"So the bullet missed?" the detective asked.

"Yes, she ducked, or—"

"What, son?"

But he was on his way out the door. "Dad," he called back over his shoulder, "be sure, lock the door on your way out. I'm going to the homes."

"What is this?" Xena was bewildered. "It doesn't even make sense! It sounds like whoever wrote it doesn't speak English very well." Most of the students at their school were British or American, but others who hadn't been in London very long sometimes had trouble with the language.

Xander grinned. "I think I figured it out. Read it out loud."

"Aha!" Xena said. "'Ducked, or, what, son, sure, lock, homes'—those words sound just like 'Dr. Watson, Sherlock Holmes'! Someone's trying to tell us they know we're related to Sherlock Holmes!"

Xander nodded.

"But why? A lot of people saw us on TV when we found that missing painting." The first case that Xena and Xander solved involved a painting that had gone missing in Sherlock Holmes's time. Xena handed the note back to her brother. "I think everybody at school knows Sherlock was our ancestor. Why wouldn't they just say something? Why the note?"

"That's what we have to find out!"

"What—*now*? It's the middle of school!"

Xander looked at the clock on the wall. "I have time. It's still my lunch hour, and I ate fast. Mom gave me tuna fish." He made a face and didn't need to say more. Xena knew how he felt about tuna. He went on. "And isn't this your free period? You said Ms. Perella doesn't care if you're late."

"Okay." Xena was eager to do a little detecting. "Let's see. Who could have been in the hallway?" She looked around at the rooms near the lockers. Science lab, teachers' lounge, janitor's closet, sixth-grade rooms.

"Almost anybody. You could tell the teacher you were going to the bathroom—"

"There aren't any bathrooms right here."

"No, but you could *say* you were going to the bathroom and then come this way."

"True." They considered. Then Xena said, "What about the paper?"

Xander examined it. "Nothing out of the ordinary. Except—what's this?" He touched the fold, and his finger stuck a bit when he pulled it away. He tried again, then sniffed at the sticky spot. "Honey!"

A hoot behind him made them turn around. It was Shane, who said in a high voice, "Yes, sweetie?"

Xander felt himself flush, but Xena laughed. "Cut it out!" Her tone was playful, and Shane grinned at her before going back to his conversation with Andrew.

"Jerk," Xander muttered.

Xena took the paper and studied the single page. She turned it over, angling it at the light. "Whoever left this wrote something else on a piece of paper on top of it and made some marks. Let's see." She squinted, her eyes close to the dents that made a light tracing over the letters. "Something about love. No, about Lord N-E-L . . ." She spelled out all the letters she could make out.

"Lord Nelson. It's got to be someone in my class! We've been studying the Battle of Trafalgar, where Lord Nelson was killed."

"Someone in your class who had honey on his or her fingers . . ."

Xander shook his head. "Sorry, I didn't stick around long enough to see who had what for dessert," he said.

Xena wasn't paying attention to him but was looking down the row of lockers. People were closing them and getting on to class, rubber-soled shoes squeaking on the polished wood floor. Only a few students were left, putting things away or taking out textbooks and note-books. Xena was good at reading body lan-guage—telling how people were feeling from the way they were walking or gesturing or even standing—and something had caught her eye.

"Do you know that guy?" She pointed at a dark-haired boy who was hanging up a jacket on the hook in his locker.

"That's Karim Farag. He's in my class. He's nice. Why?"

Xena kept her eye on the boy. "He just looks—well, he looks tense. And he took that jacket off the hook, hung it up, took it off again, and now he's hanging it up again. I think he's stalling, like he wants to stay here in the hallway for some reason."

"Let me check." Xander slung his backpack over his shoulder and went to where Karim was lingering.

The other boy looked up and nodded at Xander. He took his jacket off the hook again.

"I'm starving," Xander said to him. "I didn't

like my lunch so I hardly ate any of it. Do you have anything?"

Karim looked surprised. "My mom gave me these." He pulled a plastic bag out of his pocket. "Honey candy. My grandma made it. Want some?"

Xander felt a flush of satisfaction. "Thanks." He helped himself to a handful. "Hey, I didn't get everything Ms. Jacobsen was saying about Nelson. Can I take a look at your notes?"

Karim nodded and dropped his backpack on the floor. He rummaged around in it for a minute and then pulled out some papers. He handed them to Xander, who took one look, and then glanced at Xena and grinned. She smiled back and made her way toward them through the thinning crowd of students.

"Looks like you need a new pen," Xander said. "Yours is leaking all over the place."

Xena came up. "Okay," she said. "We know you wrote that note about Sherlock Holmes and Dr. Watson and left it in Xander's locker. What's up? If you wanted to ask him about our great-great-great grandfather, why didn't you just say something?"

Karim looked around and then beckoned them to come closer. "I had to know if you were good detectives," he whispered hoarsely. "I wanted to see if you could figure out what the note meant and that I was the one who left it. I thought that if you could find all that out, then I could trust you with something."

"Trust us with what?" Xena asked, also pitching her voice low. "Is it about whoever's been stealing things from school?"

"No, it's not about the school thief. It's about Sherlock Holmes—and a case he worked on a long time ago. He never solved it." Karim swallowed. "And I need it to be solved. I need to know what happened to—"

The bell rang. "Meet me after school!" Karim called before he hurried down the hall to his next class.

Xena and Xander watched him go in stunned silence. Finally Xena said, "Well! What do you think that's all about?"

"I don't know, but—we have another case!"

CHAPTER TWO

Karim didn't have to tell Xander where to meet him. They both had after-school soccer practice—by now Xander was used to the way it was called "football" in England—and since they'd be practicing together, Xander was sure they'd have lots of chances to talk.

But it didn't turn out that way. It was a chilly, gray day, and the coach made them run laps to warm up. Karim was one of the fastest runners on the team, and every time he slowed down to keep pace with Xander, the coach shrilled on his whistle and yelled at him.

The two boys finally managed to meet in the locker room after practice.

"So what's up?" Xander asked as he changed out of his gym clothes. "What did you mean about a case that Sherlock Holmes worked on?"

"Shh!" Karim looked around. "Not so loud! You don't know who might be listening."

Xander looked around too. "Who?"

"I don't know. But I don't want anyone to know about this. It's—it's something that other people might be interested in. Let's wait until everyone's gone."

Lockers banged, boys talked and laughed, and after what seemed like a long time, they were alone.

Or almost. The janitor, Mr. Franklin, was mopping the floor, muttering about the dirt that the boys had tracked in. "Like there's anything we can do about that," Xander grumbled. "Cleats collect an awful lot of mud." Finally Mr. Franklin and his mop and bucket moved out into the hall.

"Okay," Xander said, "but you have to be quick. They're going to lock up the school any time now."

Karim launched right into his story. "Did you ever hear of the Carberry Museum?" Xander shook his head. "It's a really small place. Some guy named Josiah S. Carberry in the eighteen hundreds had this collection of stuff, mostly fossils and bones but some art too, ancient Greek and Mesopotamian and some Egyptian things."

"Sounds cool."

"It is. Anyway, after he died his house got turned into a museum. Mr. Carberry left a lot of money, and in his will he said that the trustees, the people who run the museum, should use it to buy things that they thought he'd like."

"What are you boys still doing here?"

Xander and Karim jumped and turned around. Mr. Singh, the assistant principal, had poked his head around the open door. "Football practice," they chorused.

"This late? Well, hurry up. I have some work to do in the office, but I want to leave soon."

"Yes, sir," Karim said, and the door closed.

"So about a hundred years ago," Karim went on, "the trustees bought an Egyptian water clock. Do you know what that is?"

It had been a while since Xander had studied ancient civilization back at home, but like many people, he was fascinated with ancient Egypt. He also had the help of his photographic memory and had read most of the encyclopedia. An image popped into his head.

"It's like a big jar, right?" Karim nodded. Xander continued, "And there's a hole at the bottom and lines marked on the inside, and the Egyptians filled it with water, and as it dripped out, they could tell what time it was by the level the water reached."

"Right. There are different kinds, but that's

like the one the trustees bought. It was carved from solid rock and weighed over a ton."

Xander whistled.

"I know. It was huge. So anyway, the Egyptian government sent it here with some other things, and it arrived at a warehouse to get unpacked and cleaned, and then they were going to take it to the Carberry Museum."

"They *were* going to take it to the museum? It never got there?"

"It vanished. Overnight. Everything else the Egyptians sent was still there, but some things got messed up. A mummy had been moved, and a part of it was broken—like someone maybe was looking for something under it—but the mummy was still there. Even a gold necklace wasn't missing. Just the water clock."

"So they called in Sherlock Holmes?" Of course they would ask for help from the most famous detective of the day, and that was his ancestor! Now that he thought of it, Xander remembered seeing a drawing of something that looked like a large flowerpot in the notebook of unsolved cases that he and Xena had been given by the SPFD. That must be the water clock!

Karim sat up straighter and looked sharply to his right. "What's that?"

"What?"

"Didn't you hear something?"

Xander strained his ears. "Nope. Nothing. Don't be paranoid. Everybody's gone except Mr. Singh."

"And Mr. Franklin."

"Nah. He finished here. Hurry up—before Mr. Singh comes back."

Karim walked over to the right-hand side of the locker room, glanced toward the showers, then returned. "Nothing there. Okay." But he still seemed nervous.

"Come *on*." Xander was dying of curiosity. "What else? Why do you care about a stolen water clock? How do you even know about it?"

Karim swallowed. He appeared strangely reluctant to go on. "There were guards watching over the clock." His voice dropped even lower. "And one of them—one of the guards was my great-great-great-granduncle. And—and he confessed that he stole it."

No wonder Karim was embarrassed to talk about the theft. Xander felt sorry for him, but he was more curious than ever. If Karim's ancestor had confessed to the crime, the case was solved. So why was the theft of the clock mentioned in the notebook of Holmes's *unsolved* cases? What kind of help did Karim want? And why did he come to Xena and Xander right now? Why not months ago, when everyone first found out that they were related to the great detective who had lived a hundred years earlier?

Before Xander could ask, a few musical notes sounded from Karim's backpack. He pulled out his cell phone. "Hi, Mom. Practice ran late." He glanced anxiously at Xander. "I'm still in the locker room. No, I'm fine. Okay, five minutes. Bye." He snapped the phone shut. "I have to be quick. The water clock wasn't the only thing stolen."

"But I thought you said—"

Karim held up his hand. "Please, Xander, let me finish. I went to see my grandparents over the weekend. My granddad is ill." He gulped. "He—he was worried he was going to die, even though my dad says he'll be fine. My granddad said he had something to tell me that should be handed down from father to son. He told my father, but my father didn't believe him, so he had to tell me."

Xander felt a prickle of excitement. "What was it?"

"He told me about the water clock. He said it had a secret compartment, and inside it was a magic amulet that no one's ever found."

Xander's mind was whirring. "An amulet—you mean like a charm?" Karim nodded. "And it's *magic*?"

"That's what my granddad said." Karim lowered his voice even further and said, "Every fifty years, the amulet can make time stand still. And on Saturday"— he was practically whispering by now—"the fifty years will be up. The amulet's magic will work!"

CHAPTER THREE

For a moment Xander could only blink.

"The fifty years are up Saturday? You mean *tomorrow*?" he finally managed.

"No, a week from tomorrow. That's the day—" Karim suddenly stopped and stared to his right again, but he didn't need to say anything, because this time Xander heard the soft sound too. He leaped to his feet and dashed to the shower room, Karim right behind him. Nobody. They froze and listened with all their might. The building was old and creaky, and it was hard to tell what they heard or even what direction the noise was coming from. Were those footsteps? Maybe it was just their imagination . . . sure enough, the noises ceased.

Something on the floor caught Xander's eye. He squatted. The room was still humid, and the floor was slow to dry. It looked like—footprints. Something about them was strange. But what?

The moisture was starting to evaporate, and the faint outlines of the prints grew even dimmer. But just before the last trace disappeared, Xander realized what it was that he'd seen.

The footprint of one shoe—the right—had left an odd mark. It was a perfectly round shape, at the ball of the foot. What kind of shoe would leave a circle like that, and why wasn't it on both shoes?

Karim's phone rang again. He glanced at it. "I've got to go. Are you going to stay and investigate?"

Xander was eager to find out who had been listening to them, but he didn't like the idea of being alone in the locker room in the almost-deserted building. It was even creepier if he *wasn't* alone—if someone was lurking. What if the person who had left the strange footprint was the person who was stealing things from all the students? Xander didn't think he wanted to tangle with a thief on his own.

He didn't have to decide, though, because they heard the locker room door bang open and Mr. Singh call, "Are you chaps still here?"

The two boys sped back into the locker room and grabbed their backpacks off the bench. "Just leaving, sir," they chorused, and then, "Bye! See you Monday!"

They ran outside to where one lone car was waiting, exhaust billowing out in a cloud behind it, Karim's mother at the wheel. Xena stood waiting a little farther on, her hands in her pockets as she stamped her feet to stay warm.

Karim paused before opening the car door. "You can't tell anyone what I told you!" he said urgently.

"I have to tell my sister."

"All right, but that's all. No one else! Promise?"

Xander promised. Karim raised a hand next to his face in the sign for "call me" as he opened the door and climbed in. Xander could hear Karim's mother scolding before the door closed. He trotted over to where Xena stood on the paved walk.

"So what's up?" she asked, and then added, "Tell me on our way to the Tube station. It's freezing!"

It didn't take Xander long to fill her in. He kept glancing around to see if anyone was listening, but the school grounds were empty now. When Xander reached the part about the magic amulet having the power to make time stand still, Xena said, "Uh, wait a minute. *Magic?* Are you kidding?"

"That's what Karim said."

"And you believe him?"

Xander didn't know what to believe. "Well, even if it's not magic, it's still a missing amulet from ancient Egypt!"

They hurried down the steps to the station. They were later than usual, and the Tube station was crowded with adults going home from work, parents with their small children, and a group of what looked like high school students.

Xena cupped her hands over her ears to warm them. She and Xander had been proud to wrap up two mysteries that Sherlock Holmes had had to leave unsolved. This one didn't seem too promising, though. A magic amulet sounded weird. "Let's talk when we get home," she told her brother. "Maybe we can find something about it in the casebook."

They rode in silence, each thinking about Karim's strange story. It was growing dark and cold when they emerged from the Tube stop, but fortunately it was right near their apartment—or flat, as they'd started calling it, like their English friends. They ran up the steps and into the lift.

"We're home!" Xena called out as they let themselves in.

"About time!" Their mother came out from her study, holding an odd-looking gadget in one hand and some wires in the other. Xena and Xander didn't give the machine a second glance. They were used to their mother's job of testing products for an electronics company. "Practice ran late," Xander said. "Sorry."

"I know. Xena called me. I'd rather come pick you up if it goes this late again, okay?"

"Okay." Xander followed his sister into her bedroom, where she was already sitting on the bed, holding a large leather-bound book with the words *SH Cases: Unresolved* stamped into its worn cover. Xena opened the old journal and carefully began turning the pages covered with Sherlock's writing.

"Aha!" Xena spotted the words "water clock" in Sherlock's familiar scrawl, but the bottom half of the page was covered by an envelope tucked in between the pages. She pulled out the envelope and showed it to Xander. "What's this?"

"I don't know!" He was impatient and sounded it. "Did you find the page with the notes about the case?"

Xena tucked the envelope into the back of the book and nodded. "Here it is." She moved over, and Xander sat next to her. They examined their ancestor's notes and sketches about the theft of the water clock.

"Questioned guard named Amin for two hours. Confessed to—nay, bragged about—the crime. Motive?

"Other Egyptian guard claims amulet hidden in water clock. Mentions Tahuti.

"Trustees say that amulet would be very valuable. They don't believe in it, but guard seems credible.

"Egyptian magic? Poppycock!

"Case dropped by order of HIM, as being potentially damaging to relations with Egypt. Drat!"

"So there *was* an amulet!" Xander said.

"I never said there wasn't. I just don't know if I believe in this magic stuff."

"I don't know if I do either, but even an amulet that *wasn't* magic would be cool."

"See? 'Poppycock!' Sherlock didn't believe in the magic part either!" Xena said. She pointed at a drawing of a hand with an eye on its palm. "Is that a tattoo?"

"Could be. Or maybe just a doodle."

"So someone named Amin confessed to stealing the water clock." As usual, Xena had to muster the facts.

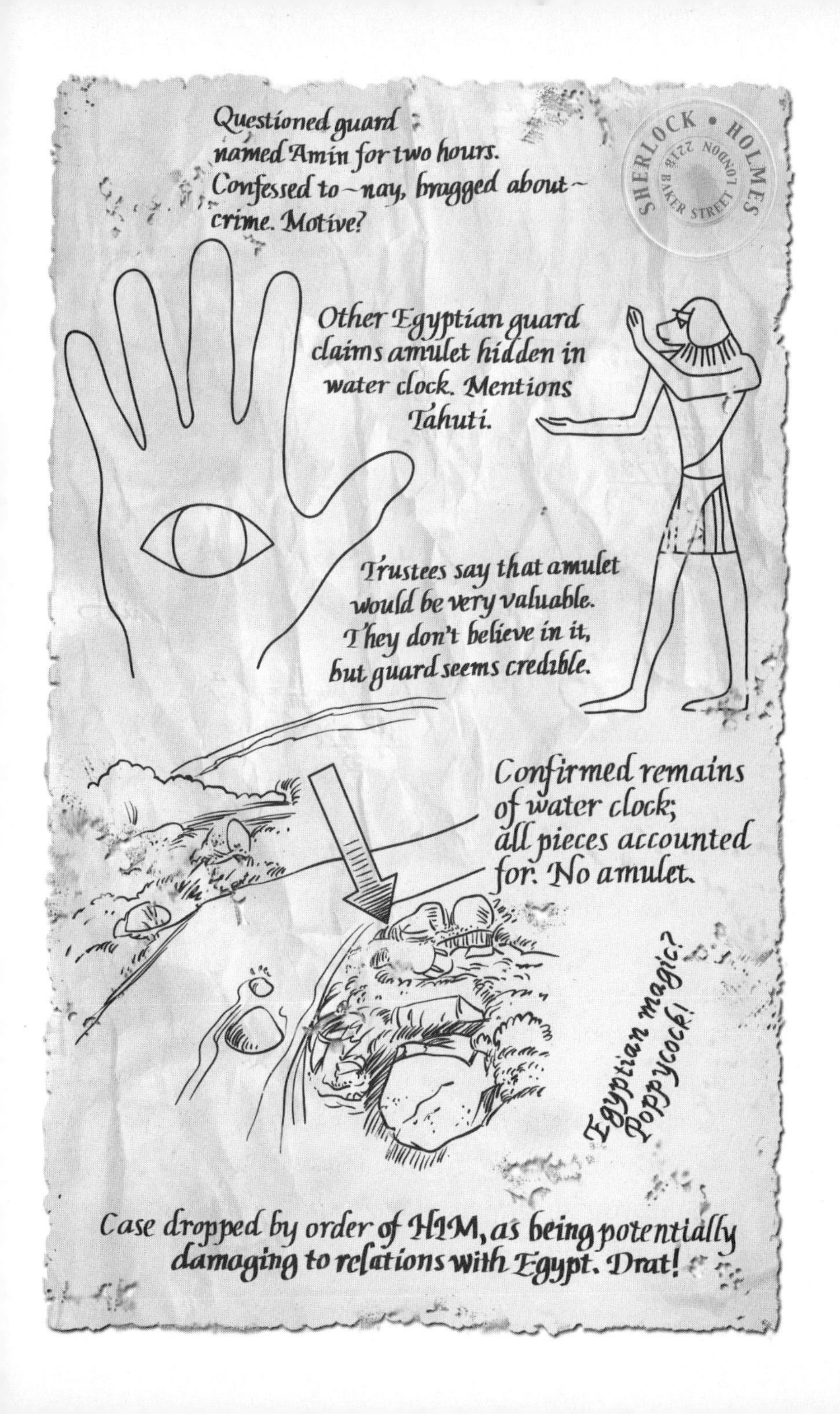
Questioned guard
named Amin for two hours.
Confessed to ~ nay, bragged about ~
crime. Motive?
SHERLOCK • HOLMES
LONDON 221B
BAKER STREET
Other Egyptian guard
claims amulet hidden in
water clock. Mentions
Tahuti.
Trustees say that amulet
would be very valuable.
They don't believe in it,
but guard seems credible.
Confirmed remains
of water clock;
all pieces accounted
for. No amulet.
Egyptian magic?
Poppycock!
Case dropped by order of HIM, as being potentially
damaging to relations with Egypt. Drat!

"Right."

"And he must be that kid's—"

"Karim."

"He must be Karim's great-great-great-granduncle," Xena said. "And there was some other guard who told Sherlock and the Carberry people about the amulet, but Sherlock didn't believe it was magic."

Xander frowned. "It looks like he wasn't one hundred percent certain the amulet existed."

"No, he was sure about *that*. Otherwise he wouldn't have left notes about it in his cold-case notebook. If the case was only about the missing water clock, he would have said the case was closed. Something was still unsolved. It had to be the part about the amulet—Sherlock believed there was an amulet, and it was still missing."

"Oh, right." Xander felt a flutter of excitement. If Sherlock Holmes thought that the amulet had existed, then surely it had! Where was it now? And how could they find it?

"It doesn't look like we have a lot to go on," Xena said.

"There's one more thing." Xander told her about his suspicion that someone had been listening to his conversation with Karim. He sketched the odd footprint from the shower floor on a page of the small notebook he always carried with him.

"I don't know." Xena inspected it, her head tilted to one side as she thought. "That's not much."

"Sherlock would have continued with the case. He only dropped it because some guy asked him to. See? 'Case dropped by order of HIM, as being potentially damaging to relations with Egypt.'"

"That wasn't just *someone*! That was the queen!"

"The queen wasn't a him!"

Xena sighed. "No, dope. It's all capitals. See? It stands for 'Her Imperial Majesty.' Queen Victoria was the ruler of England then."

"Oh. Well, that's different. If the queen ordered Sherlock to drop the case, he wouldn't have a choice."

Xena still looked unconvinced.

"Let's at least talk to Karim and ask what he wants," Xander suggested. "Maybe he can help. He might know more than what the casebook says. Maybe he has some clues! He asked me to call him, anyway."

When Xander finally managed to find

Karim's cell number, Karim couldn't talk. "I'm having supper," he said. "Can you come for tea tomorrow? We can give you a ride over here after the football match. You and your sister too, of course. I already asked my mother. *Do* come. I'll tell you all about it then. I really need your help *now*."

It turned out that their mother had met Karim's mother a few times and liked her, so she said it was fine for them to go.

"We can come," Xander reported. "See you at the match!"

"See you!" Karim sounded relieved. "And, Xander—there's more I can tell you about the amulet. Lots more."

CHAPTER FOUR

Xander woke to the sound of Xena arguing with their father. *Oh, no,* he groaned inwardly. What if she said something that got her grounded?

He dressed quickly and saw that the sun was shining feebly. Good—maybe the weather would be better for the match. He pushed open the kitchen door to see his sister with her fists on her hips. She was saying, "But, Dad, the school is only a fifteen-minute drive! It takes almost forty minutes if I have to go on the Tube!"

"That's half an hour there and back." Their father was reading the newspaper, a cup of coffee in his hand. He looked over the paper at Xander and said, "There's some hot cereal on the stove for you."

Xander filled his bowl, and their father went on. "Have you started your science project yet?"

"My *science* project?" Xena's voice was shrill with disbelief. "But, Dad, it's Saturday! And the project isn't due for almost two weeks!"

"You need to at least choose the topic today," he said. "And then I'll take you to Xander's match. One round trip to school is enough for today. It's my day off too, you know."

Xena stomped to her room while Xander gulped down his oatmeal. When he finished, he knocked on her door, but she told him to go away.

Xena didn't talk the whole way to school, and as soon as the car stopped, she got out without saying good-bye to their dad and ran up to the bleachers to sit with Hannah, Shane, and Jake. She must be really mad about missing the earlier match when Jake and Shane were playing, Xander thought.

During his game Xander kept glancing up into the stands, but Xena wasn't even pretending to watch him play and didn't notice when he scored a goal. Her attention was fixed on her friends.

What was so great about them, anyway? Jake was okay, but Shane was one of those people who treated younger kids like they were invisible, and Hannah didn't seem to notice or care. But Xander knew the three of them were the cool kids of his sister's grade.

Up in the stands, Xena felt awkward.

Hannah and Shane were talking mostly to each other, and she didn't know Jake very well.

"So what brings you to London?" he asked. Jake had a friendly face under his tousled brown hair.

"My dad's job," she explained. "He's a music teacher, and one of his old friends is in the music department at the university. His friend is on leave this year, and he recommended my dad as his replacement."

"My mum teaches at the university too!" Jake exclaimed. "Maybe they know each other!" Then his face clouded over as though he was worried about something.

Before Xena could ask him what was the matter, Shane turned to her and said, "Where's your magnifying glass?"

"My—what do you mean?"

"I thought you were related to Sherlock Holmes."

Xena nodded, still mystified.

"So every time you see a picture of him he's holding a magnifying glass and smoking a pipe. Do you smoke a pipe?"

"Of course not." Xena was indignant. "And the pictures show him with a magnifying glass because that's about the only piece of equipment he used. He figured out his cases with just his brain."

"Not like you and your brother! You couldn't do a thing without your computer."

Xena flushed. "We use our brains too," she said coldly. "The computer and metal detector and other things we've used speed things up, but we figure out the solutions to our cases mostly without them."

"Your cases!" Shane hooted. "Don't you mean—?"

"Weren't you going to get me some cocoa, Shane?" Hannah broke in. She smiled at him, and Shane got up reluctantly and headed down to the concession stand. Before he got back, the game ended, and Hannah and Jake went to join Shane.

Xena waited on the paved walk for Xander and Karim. It was still cold, and she refused an offer of a lift from Shane's father, who was instantly recognizable from his resemblance to his son, crew cut and all. She passed up another ride from Jake and his mother, a tall woman dressed in a lab coat. Xena was stamping her feet to stay warm when the two younger boys finally emerged. She would be glad when soccer season was finally over!

• • •

"So what's Egyptian food like?" Xena asked as they hung their coats on hooks inside the door to the Farags' flat. "I've never tried it."

"And I'm afraid you won't be trying it today," said the short, dark-haired woman who came out of the kitchen wiping her hands on her apron. "Karim wanted all his favorite things for tea, and that means sandwiches and jam cake. If I'd known you wanted Egyptian food, I would have been happy to make you some."

"Oh, I'm sure sandwiches and cake will be fine," Xena said hastily.

Karim's mother said, "Well, you'll just have to come back sometime, and we'll have an Egyptian feast! I love to cook the food from home, but Karim is completely an English boy, I'm afraid."

The sandwiches were delicious, and Karim's parents were fun. His mother asked them a lot of questions about life in Florida, and his father, a lawyer, liked to tease.

Karim's little sister, Dalia, a small girl with large brown eyes, seemed fascinated with Xander. She finished eating before everyone else and got whiny, and nothing would make her happy except to sit in Xander's lap.

"You're just going to have to move in!" Mr. Farag said with a laugh.

"Oh, he charms everybody!" Xena said.

"Even spoiled little girls," Mrs. Farag said as she lifted the sleepy child off Xander and carried her away for a nap.

When they were through eating, Xena and Xander helped Karim clear the table. The three of them went into the sitting room, which was cheery and comfortable, with modern furniture, large abstract paintings in bright colors, and big windows with a view of a park.

"Finally!" Xander said. "Now *please* tell us what you know about the amulet!"

CHAPTER FIVE

Have a seat," Karim said. "I'll be back in a sec." He went out of the room while Xander sat on a wooden chair and Xena settled herself on the carpet in front of a low metal-and-glass table.

Karim reappeared carrying a tan folder. "My dad gave me this when I asked him about what my granddad said." He put it down on the table in front of Xena. "Go ahead, take a look."

The folder held a few yellowed newspaper clippings. Xena glanced at Karim and then picked up the top one and inspected it. "Wow, this is more than a hundred years old!" Xander got down from his chair and joined her on the floor, sneezing at the musty smell.

Xena passed the first clipping to Xander. Xander could scan print so quickly that she sometimes couldn't believe it, and once he read something it would be in his memory forever—or at least for six years. They hadn't tested any further than that—he'd learned to read at age four, six years ago, and hadn't forgotten anything yet.

"This one's about when they found the water clock," Xander said after a quick look. "It was smashed into pieces on the riverbank near the museum."

"By the river," Xena mused. "I wonder if the thieves were planning to take it someplace on a boat—like back to Egypt—and then they dropped it."

Xander shook his head as he scanned the page. "Nope. Sherlock inspected the pieces and said that it had been busted up on purpose, not by being dropped. According to the article, that part of the river was pretty marshy. It looks like it was the closest place to the warehouse where the thieves could smash the water clock without being seen."

"Right," Karim said. "People wouldn't go someplace like that for a stroll."

"What does the next clipping say?" Xena asked.

"It says that this guy Amin was missing, and they thought that maybe he'd been murdered. Other people said no, he was the thief and had run away. Sherlock said," Xander read from the article, "'The truth will out! I will find him and bring him to justice. It is for the law to say whether he was a thief, an accomplice, an innocent bystander, or an unfortunate victim. I am but a servant of the law.'"

"Wow!" Xena was delighted to find a direct quote from their ancestor.

Xander quickly scanned the rest of the article and put it down. He held out his hand, and Xena put another clipping in it.

"One week later," he noted. "Okay, here it says that Sherlock found Amin. He'd been hiding with someone who lived in London but refused to say who. It also says—" His voice changed, and Xena could tell he was excited. "It says that when Sherlock searched Amin, he found a piece of paper on him."

"Was anything written on it?" Xena leaned forward.

Xander's face showed his disappointment. "It doesn't say." He shook his head and put down the clipping. "Must not have been anything important."

"That's what I thought at first," Karim said eagerly. "But then I thought about it. I think that it *was* important, and Mr. Holmes asked the reporters not to say what it said. It must have been something about where the amulet was hidden, and I bet Mr. Holmes didn't want anyone to find it before he had a chance to look for it."

Xander ran his eye over another clipping. "Hmm."

"What does it say?" Xena tried not to sound impatient. Honestly, Xander could be so annoying.

This time Xander read the short account aloud. "'The other Egyptian guard, whose name has not been released, has revealed to this reporter that Mr. Amin Farag boasted that as the descendant of an ancient priesthood, he had privileged knowledge that hidden inside the basin of the clock was a rare and beautiful amulet of Thoth, the ancient Egyptian god of time and timekeeper of the gods, made of gold and precious gems.'" He took a breath. "Phew, they wrote long sentences back then!"

"What else?" Xena asked.

"'Mr. Holmes has been apprised of this fact and has said that he had already deduced that the clock had been stolen in order to permit access to its interior, and perhaps to something concealed there. He expresses himself eager to pursue further this intriguing story.'"

Xander looked at the folder. "Where's the next clipping?"

"There isn't one," Karim said.

"So what happened next?" Xena asked. "Did Amin go to jail?"

Karim shook his head. "My granddad says that the Egyptian government was embarrassed about the whole thing. The Carberry Museum bought the water clock fair and square, and then their own employee stole it and destroyed it. So they asked for Amin to be sent back to Egypt so that they could have a trial, and then Mr. Holmes stopped working on the case."

He sounded hurt, as though he had personally been abandoned by the great detective.

Xena said quickly, "He didn't want to. He had to. The queen made him stop. Sherlock didn't forget about it, though. He kept the records in his cold-case notebook."

"I wonder why the Egyptian government let Amin come to England with the water clock," Xander said.

"They didn't know about the priesthood thing, I bet," Karim said. "Amin worked for the archaeologist who found the water clock, and he asked if he could be one of the guards who went with it to England so that he could visit his brother after they got the water clock delivered."

"Amin's brother was your great-great-great-grandfather?" Xena asked.

Karim nodded. "He was already living in London. That's who Amin stayed with when he was hiding from the police. And that's when Amin told my great-great-great grandfather about the amulet, and he told his son the whole story, and he told his son, and he told *his* son, and my granddad told me."

"What else did your grandfather tell you?" Xander wanted to know.

"He said that Amin was angry with the Egyptian government for selling the water clock, so he confessed to taking it. He was even proud of his crime."

"Why was he so upset about the sale?" Xena asked. "Was the clock really rare?"

"No," Karim said. "Of course anything from ancient Egypt is valuable, but there are other water clocks around, and they didn't think there was anything special about this one. Amin must have been angry because he couldn't get to the amulet. If it was in a museum in England, he'd never be able to find it and take it back to Egypt with him, or whatever it was he wanted to do."

Xena took a deep breath. Now for the hard part. "Karim, do you really believe that the amulet can make time stand still?"

Karim lifted his chin. "I do." His voice was

stubborn. "That's what my grandfather told me, and he should know."

"So how's it supposed to work?" Xander asked. "Do you have to say something in ancient Egyptian? Do you even *know* any ancient Egyptian?"

Karim shook his head. "My granddad says that all you have to do is hold the amulet. You hold it in your hand, and you concentrate really hard, and time stops."

"And how do you make it go again?" Xena had a moment of wondering what it would be like if everything stopped except you, and then you couldn't make time start moving again. Would you wander around frozen people forever, watching them stay the same as you got old and eventually died? *Would* you die? Could you even eat and drink if the water and food were stuck in time and you weren't?

"All you have to do is put the amulet down, and time starts up. He says they used it in the olden days during a ritual to the god of time, Thoth. But it works only once every fifty years."

It sounded crazy, but Karim seemed to believe it, and Karim was a sensible person. For the first time, Xena seriously considered the possibility of stopping time.

"Wow." Xander finally spoke. "Imagine if you're in a football game. You could make time stop while you got in the right place to make a goal."

"Or if you had a big project due at school," Xena said, intrigued despite her skepticism, "and it's due in two weeks and you haven't started it. You could get it all done in time!"

Xander said to Karim, "We looked in Sherlock's casebook, the one we got from the SPFD—"

"The what?"

"The Society for the Preservation of Famous Detectives," Xena explained. "They're a group of people who want to keep the memory of famous detectives from the past alive. They gave us the casebook, and they have a lab and know all sorts of experts. You know Andrew Watson at school?" Karim nodded. "Andrew belongs to the SPFD too. His great-great-great grandfather was Sherlock's best friend, Dr. Watson. Anyway, the casebook has some notes in it, but they're mostly about the water clock, not the amulet. Sherlock didn't get much of a chance to investigate the amulet."

Karim glanced quickly to the hallway, where they could hear his parents talking to each other, and lowered his voice. "My dad told my granddad he thinks it's silly that I believe all this. That hurt my granddad's feelings, so he gave me something else that he said would prove it. I don't know, though—I don't understand it."

"What is it?" Xander breathed.

The other boy stood and took his wallet from his back pocket. He pulled out yet another yellowing piece of paper. He spread it on the table. This time it wasn't newsprint, but only a few handwritten words. The old-fashioned writing was so faint that it was hard to read, even more so because Xena and Xander were looking at it upside down.

"What's this?" Xena asked. The back of her neck prickled.

Karim lowered his voice. "My granddad said that when his own grandfather was a little boy, a letter came from Egypt. There was a note in it that said, 'Here begins the trail,' and then this piece of paper."

"The *trail*? What trail?" Xena asked.

"Oh, Xena, what does it matter?" Xander was dying to know what the paper said. "Let's read it first and then we can figure out what 'the trail' means. What does it say, Karim?"

Karim picked up the paper and read solemnly, "Who Bastet rules, she Bastet rules. The secret must be held to the sun."

CHAPTER SIX

Silence. Then, "O-kay," Xander said slowly. "Who Bastet rules—"

"She Bastet rules. The secret must be held to the sun," Xena finished for him. "And this is some kind of trail?"

"I don't know what it means," Karim confessed. "That's why I had to ask you, don't you see? This letter was sent after Mr. Holmes died, so he never saw it. But it's got to be a clue about the amulet."

Xena and Xander looked at each other. There had to be more than this.

Karim went on, "My great-great-grandfather hired a detective to trace the letter so that he could find Amin and ask him what it meant, but when he finally found the right village in Egypt, it turned out that Amin had died right after he sent it."

"So you're not sure—" Xena began.

"My granddad told me that Amin hid the amulet somewhere in London and left clues for his descendants to find," Karim said. "He's sure this note is one of those clues. My granddad wants the amulet to be found before he dies. He knows my father doesn't believe in it, so when he saw you on the news after you found that missing painting and I told him I knew Xander, he asked me to see if you could help."

"You kids are being awfully quiet!" All three jumped as Karim's father came into the room. "Why don't you play a game or something? I'll have to run Xena and Xander home before long." His eye fell on the piece of paper. He picked it up. "What's this?"

Karim explained. His father frowned at the paper, then sighed and put it down. "It's nice of you two to want to help. Karim is very close to his grandfather, and I know he believes this whole tale." He held up his hand as Karim started to say something. Karim sat back and crossed his arms over his chest, looking out the window instead of at his father, who continued, "My father is a wonderful storyteller. I think the tale of the magic amulet is something he made up to amuse his children and grandchildren. Anyway, even if it *is* true and if Amin left hints about the amulet's location, they've been lost. My father said that when my great-great-granduncle was arrested, Mr. Holmes found some clues on him, but nobody knows what happened to them."

Xander started to say something but bit his tongue. Xena looked at him sharply.

"Why would he tell Mr. Holmes there was a hidden amulet if there wasn't?" Karim broke in.

"Our ancestor must have been taunting Holmes with that tale about the amulet. Now, Karim, why don't you three stop talking about this and do something fun before I have to take your guests home?"

Xena and Xander were itching to consult the casebook. When Karim's father came back half an hour later and told them it was time to leave, they thanked Mrs. Farag, said good-bye to Dalia (who hugged Xander tightly around the neck), and followed Mr. Farag out to his car. Karim came along for the ride. It wasn't very late, but the days were so short that it was pitch-dark outside.

Karim's father let them out in front of their apartment building.

"Would you like to come in?" Xena asked.

"Thanks, but we have to get back." Mr. Farag and Karim sat in the car and watched as they climbed the steps to their building.

Was it just because it was dark and the streets were nearly empty that they felt uneasy? Xena was careful to pull the door shut tight behind them and to hear the lock click. Once they were safely inside the lift, she asked Xander, "What were you going to say back there?"

"When?"

"Remember—when Mr. Farag said that about the paper found on Amin?"

"Oh, right," Xander said. "The missing clue! I think we have it!"

They ran into the living room, only to stop short at the sight of their parents and another couple sitting there while two small children played on the rug. The adults looked up.

"What's the hurry?" their father asked. "Xena and Xander, you remember Mr. and Mrs. Sanderson from downstairs, don't you?"

"Yes, I babysat for them once, remember?" Xena said as they stepped forward to shake hands.

"Of course!" their mother said. "And guess what—we're all going out to dinner."

"What, *now*?" Xena asked, and the adults laughed, which made her flush.

"Yes, now! You're usually starving!" her mother said.

They ate at a Chinese restaurant, and then the much younger Sylvia and Brian were so full of energy that they all went for a walk in the dark, damp evening.

"Don't they have a bedtime?" Xander whispered to Xena as the two children ran ahead.

"Spoiled rotten," Xena whispered back. "They stay up as late as they want."

By the time they got home, it was much too late to do any detecting. They tried to stay up later than their parents, but they were both so exhausted that they fell fast asleep.

The next morning, Xena woke before Xander. She ate a quick breakfast and was soon perched in front of the family's one computer in the sitting room, where she did a search for "Bastet."

"Also known as Bast, this Egyptian goddess is usually represented as a slender woman with the head of a cat," Xena read. "Protectress of Lower (northern) Egypt, Bastet was a fierce war goddess and originally goddess of the sun (later the moon as Egypt became influenced by Greece and its female moon deity)."

"Who Bastet rules . . . ," she said out loud.

"What?" her mother asked.

"Nothing," Xena mumbled. Did this mean

they had to go to Lower Egypt? Or the moon? Where else would Bastet rule? She remembered the other strange word in the casebook—"Tahuti"—and looked that up too. It was another name for Thoth, who turned out to be the god of magic, writing, and justice, as well as time. Thoth was sometimes represented as an ibis—a waterbird with a long beak—and sometimes as a baboon.

Xander finally appeared. While he went to get breakfast, Xena grabbed the casebook out of his room and spread it open on the table.

Xander wolfed down his breakfast and came back as Xena was leafing through the book. He sat next to her and said through his last mouthful of toast, "Those strange things about Tahuti and the drawing of the hand must be things that Amin said to Sherlock. They've got to be clues."

"Or maybe Amin just made them up and was messing with Sherlock." Xena was still skeptical. "Or maybe Karim's father is right and it's all just a story."

Xander wiped the jam off his fingers and took the book from Xena. "Here, let me show you," he said as he flipped to the end. He pulled out the envelope that Xena had tucked into the binding when they were looking at the casebook earlier. "Aha! Before you moved it, this was stuck right in the pages where he wrote about the missing amulet, remember? And look." He pointed at the faint letters on the flap. "A. F.—Amin Farag! I saw those initials, but I didn't pay any attention. It's got to be the paper that Sherlock found on Amin."

Xena stared at him. "How can you be so sure?"

"We looked at everything in the casebook when we first got it, remember?"

"Sort of, but—"

"But we didn't pay much attention to the note in the envelope, because it didn't make sense to us then."

Xander drew the thin slip of paper out of the envelope and unfolded it. It appeared ready to crumble at any moment. "The handwriting is familiar," he said. "It was written by the same person who wrote that thing about Bastet."

"What does it say?" Xena tried to read over his shoulder. Xander read aloud:

"I am a needle but cannot sew.
I have no eye and cannot see.
I face my sister across the sea,
and toward my sister you must go."

I am a needle but cannot sew,
I have no eye and cannot see,
I face my sister across the sea,
and toward my sister you must go.

500 yards from
monument on riverbank

Below that was written *500 yards from monument on riverbank* in the same handwriting, followed by Egyptian hieroglyphs.

It still didn't make much sense, Xena thought. A needle that can't sew, an eye that can't see?

"The London Eye?" she guessed, thinking of the huge Ferris wheel on the bank of the Thames River.

Xander shook his head. "That wasn't built until 1999, way after Amin died. Besides," he pointed out, "we need a needle without an eye, not an eye without a needle. What about a Cyclops? It's missing an eye."

Xena gave him a withering look. "They could see, plus, they're *Greek* mythology. And what do they have to do with needles?"

"Okay, okay. Something about that eye in the casebook, the one that looked like it was tattooed on a hand?"

They gave it some thought, but this didn't seem to get them anywhere. This case was discouraging. They kept finding clues, but they had no idea what they meant.

"Time for a list." Xena drew a piece of paper toward her and uncapped a pen. "We have to get organized about this." She made two columns and headed one QUESTIONS and the other ANSWERS. Under QUESTIONS she wrote:

1. Can the amulet really make time stand still?

"I don't think we can prove that until we find it." Xander was careful not to say "unless." He didn't want to jinx this investigation—it was hard enough already! Xena put a question mark in the ANSWERS column.

2. What happened to the amulet after it was stolen?

"If Amin found the amulet when he smashed the clock, he must have hidden it away for safe-keeping," Xena said. "He must have planned to come back for it later, or surely it would have surfaced by now. Even if that stuff about making time stand still isn't true, it's supposed to have jewels on it and a museum would love to have it. It must still be in its hiding place." Another question mark.

3. What do the hieroglyphs on the page with the riddle mean?

Xander said, "That's one we can get to work on, finally! Let's send it to Andrew. Someone at the SPFD must know an expert who can translate the hieroglyphs for us."

"Good idea." Xena turned back to the computer, typed a quick note explaining the situation, and e-mailed it to Andrew. "Next," she said, returning to her list.

4. Who Bastet rules?

"What was that whole thing, again?" Xena asked.

"'Who Bastet rules, she Bastet rules. The secret must be held to the sun,'" Xander recited.

Xena wrote the words on a scrap of paper and tucked it into the casebook. Xander rolled his eyes at her. "Hey, I don't have your photographic memory!" she said, and put another question mark in the ANSWERS column, then continued writing.

5. Needle without an eye?

Xena didn't even bother with the ANSWERS column for this one. Instead she said, "I'm going to do some research about needles and eyes. Why don't you see if Mom has anything that we can use in our investigation?"

She returned to the computer while Xander rooted around in the box of gadgets their mother kept after she evaluated them. You never knew what might come in handy. Who would have thought that a metal detector would help them find a painting that had been missing for a century, or that a tape recorder would lead them to a savage beast in the countryside? Plus, there was usually something cool in the box.

First Xander found some night-vision goggles. Fun but hardly useful, as their parents wouldn't let them go out after dark by themselves. Headphones that you could use to eavesdrop on someone a long way away—were those even legal for someone who wasn't a policeman? Xander wasn't sure so he put them back. A hologram projector. He puzzled over the instruction manual until he discovered that it was a way to make a three-dimensional image appear and seem to be actually present with you. Way cool but not very helpful. He set it aside to try out some Halloween.

Their mother came out of her study. She was used to her kids rummaging through her gadget box and even encouraged them to do so, since she liked to be able to test how sturdy the devices were.

"What's this?" Xander held up something that looked like a wristwatch.

She took it from him. "Oh, this is a voice-activated GPS system. It can tell you where you are and give you directions, but the screen is too small to be useful. There's not much point to a map if you can't read it."

Xander strapped it on, and after it booted up,

he tested it. The screen was indeed small, but he had no trouble reading it. "You should have used your reading glasses!" he teased his mother.

"You just wait!" she said with a laugh. "Someday you'll need help reading fine print and threading a needle!"

From the computer, Xena asked, "What's a needle without an eye, anyway?"

"A knitting needle?" their mother guessed. Xena and Xander thought a minute and then shook their heads.

"A needle without an eye is just a pin," Xander said. "But what's so special about a pin?"

Just then the phone rang next to Xena. "Hello?" Nothing. "Hello?" she repeated, a bit louder.

She was about to hang up when a voice said huskily, "You'd better stop looking for it now, or you'll be sorry." Before she could say anything, the line went dead.

CHAPTER SEVEN

Xena stared at the phone in disbelief.

"Who was it?" Mrs. Holmes asked.

Xena shook her head. "I don't know." She repeated the caller's words to her mother.

"Where did the call come from?" Xander asked. Xena glanced down at the caller ID. The word BLOCKED stared back at her.

"Did you recognize the voice?" their mother asked.

Xena shook her head. "It sounded like the caller was trying to disguise it." Something about the voice was familiar, though. Where had she heard it before? She concentrated but could not remember. This was frustrating; she had a good memory for sounds.

"Let me have the phone," her mother said.

Xander pulled Xena aside as their mother made a call. "Did it sound like a kid or a grown-up?" he asked.

"Hard to tell. A kid, I guess." Their mom had been so distracted she hadn't even asked that question, or, for that matter, what the caller meant by "you'd better stop looking for it."

"All right. Thanks. Can you let me know if you find out anything?" their mother said into the phone. She hung up and said to them, "The phone company is going to contact the police, but they're not optimistic about tracing the call. It didn't last long enough. I wouldn't worry about it, though. It sounds like the kind of prank call kids make." But Xena and Xander both noticed that she looked more worried than she sounded.

Xena and Xander went into Xena's room. "So someone knows about the amulet!" Xander said. "It must be the same person who was hiding in the locker room."

"And he—or she—must want us to stop the investigation. There's only one reason for that."

"Our spy wants to find it before we do," Xander said in a grim voice.

Xena nodded. "And we can't let that happen. Let's see what we can find out about water clocks. Maybe we'll get a clue there." She got on the computer again and typed "Egyptian water clock" into a search engine. Lots of sites came up, but one caught her interest. "Xander, check this out."

He came over and looked at the screen. "The Timekeepers Museum—and it's right here in London! Maybe someone there knows something that could help."

"Not today, though. It's Sunday, remember?"

Xander flung himself down on the couch. "How could I forget? Less than a week left! We can't just sit here all day!"

"We can go to the Timekeepers Museum tomorrow after school. Let's plan our trip there so that we don't waste any time." Xena clicked back to the museum's home page and read the address off the screen.

"I bet I'll find the Tube stop before you!" Xander pulled his trusty map out of his pocket, the one that their mother had given him shortly after their arrival in London and that showed some of the most famous tourist attractions in the city. He used it so much that it was frayed and the creases were split.

"Beat you!" Xena said. "I'm sending them an e-mail asking if we can find out about water clocks there."

But Xander wasn't listening. Something not far from their destination had caught his eye. It was the drawing of an Egyptian sphinx, and it was right on the edge of the Thames River. "Xena! Look at this!"

She finished writing the e-mail and clicked SEND. She got up and stretched. "What?"

He pointed. She looked at the sphinx and then at him. "So what?"

"Don't you remember? The clue about the monument on the river!"

"I don't know." She was doubtful, as usual. "It's not really a monument."

"Oh, come *on*, Xena. You're just saying that because I found it and you didn't! It's big, it's Egyptian, and it's right on the river. And anyway, it's really near that Timekeepers place. We can go there afterward."

The sun was shining weakly the next afternoon as they stood outside the Timekeepers Museum in Guildhall, a part of London that Xena and Xander didn't know very well. They pushed the door open and saw a long, dimly lit room full of tall glass cases that held a collection of clocks made of polished wood and brass.

They stopped at the front desk to pick up a guide to the collection. "We're not getting many people today, I'm afraid," the man at the desk told them. "Not everybody is as interested in these things as you are. You have the place almost to yourselves!"

The cases held beautiful clocks and watches of all kinds. In one case marked CURIOSITIES, big pocket watches dangled from heavy gold chains. Cuckoo clocks with intricate carvings stood next to delicate watches and an alarm clock with two large, almost flat bells on top. "They look like the ones in cartoons," Xander said. "You know, the ones that jump around when they ring."

Xena admired a clock whose cover was made of glass so you could see the movement inside. It was precise and orderly, just as she liked.

The man who had let them in came up to where Xander stood looking at a case that held a special exhibit of ancient timepieces. "Not much good at night!" The man gestured at the sundial that stood in the center.

"So is that why they invented these?" Xander leaned closer to peer at the water clocks, hourglasses, and candles that had lines marked on them telling what time it was when the flame burned down to that point.

The man nodded as Xena joined them. "Yes, you could use them even when the sun was down or on a cloudy day. Some of them were quite precise, but others gave only a rough idea of the time. Are you the children who were interested in Egyptian timekeeping?"

"That's us," Xena said. "So you got my e-mail?"

"Yes, I read it when I arrived at work this morning. I'm Mr. Grayson. I found some material for you in the library. Come with me."

In his bright and cheery office was a pile of books with colorful sticky notes poking out in several places. Mr. Grayson opened the books, one after the other, to show them photographs and line drawings of water clocks. "The drip holes were drilled to very exact specifications," he told them. "But imagine what would happen if a bug or even some dust fell into it and plugged it up!"

Mr. Grayson opened another book. This one was old, and the pages with photographs on them were covered with thin sheets of tissue paper that had become imprinted with a ghostly copy of the image on the other page. One photograph of a huge bowl shaped like a flowerpot and made of pale-colored stone, was captioned "The Thoth Clock."

Xander instantly recognized it from the broken pieces of the water clock from the casebook! "What's this?" he asked.

The Thoth Clock

Mr. Grayson sighed. "What a shame. It was smashed over a hundred years ago."

Xena nudged Xander, who nudged her back.

"It was broken before anyone had a chance really to examine it," Mr. Grayson went on. "We do know a few things about it, though, because in the nineteen fifties a similar clock was found, and scientists discovered a hole drilled right here." He put his finger under a seated figure that was so battered it was unidentifiable. "It was capped with a piece of stone so perfectly made that you couldn't see a seam."

"Was there anything in the hole?" Xena asked eagerly.

"Not that we know of," Mr. Grayson said.

Xena felt a flash of excitement. That sounded exactly like a hiding place for something small, like the amulet, especially if it was hidden by a carving of a baboon, one of the ways that Thoth was pictured. And if it had been that perfectly made, no wonder the people in the Carberry Museum hadn't seen it. They hadn't had the chance to make a thorough examination, and even if they had, they might not have found the little hole with the limited technology of a century ago.

Xena and Xander thanked Mr. Grayson and walked out into the chilly afternoon. They turned right on Upper Thames Street and made their way to the wide gray river, walking past several bridges, until they paused on the Victoria Embankment near Charing Cross. Traffic whizzed past them, so they went into the small park, where a huge column with squared-off sides and a pointed top loomed above them.

"Look!" Xander flung his hand triumphantly at the two sphinxes at the base of the column.

"Wow!" Xena walked over and admired them.

A tour group came up, the man in front holding a bright yellow flag. The group of chatting people who followed gathered in a small group to hear him.

"Clear off, you kids," he said to Xena and Xander. "This tour is for paying customers only."

Xander moved away, but Xena stayed put. She knew that if she held still, she'd manage to blend in with the crowd and hear what he had to say. This was a talent she'd always had, and she found it useful in situations like this one.

"The two sphinxes here still show the effects of the German bombs dropped on them in the Second World War," the tour guide said, and then he droned on with facts about the sphinxes' weight, how old they were, and what the writing on them meant.

Xena caught a glimpse of someone lurking around the monument. She shifted her position to get a better look, but he ducked into the crowd. Xander didn't seem to notice the shadowy figure, and she knew that if she said something, the tour guide would see her and make her leave. She kept one eye on her brother while she turned the rest of her attention to the guide.

"Now, this obelisk," the man said, pointing to the column, "was brought here from Egypt in 1877. It weighs a hundred and eighty tons. Although it was made fifteen hundred years before the birth of the Egyptian queen Cleopatra, it has always been jokingly referred to as Cleopatra's Needle."

Xena gasped. A needle—but without an eye! And it had been there well before Amin had come to London. This *must* be the needle in the riddle! She looked around for Xander, only to see him frantically waving to get her attention. As soon as he saw her looking at him, he pointed to a stand of trees. She spotted someone in a dark hooded sweatshirt and jeans, before whoever it was darted out of the shelter of the trees and sped toward the sidewalk. Xena squeezed through the crowd and sprinted after him.

She paused and looked around. Where had he

gone? Then out of the corner of her eye, she saw someone running away at full speed down the sidewalk. Hooded sweatshirt, jeans—it was the same person! She took off again, dodging people and dogs and baby carriages. The person ahead of her tore through a crosswalk just as the light changed. Horns beeped and brakes squealed, but her quarry leaped onto the sidewalk on the other side and disappeared into the crowd.

Xena leaned over, hands on knees, to catch her breath. The person she was chasing had blended in with the other people going home or shopping, and by the time the light changed, he—or she?—would be far, far away.

When Xena could breathe regularly again, she turned back to the park. She found Xander standing near the trees where the mysterious figure had first appeared. "Too late," she said.

"Not entirely!" Xander pointed at the ground. In the mud were two perfect footprints. Xander pulled the notebook out of his back pocket and flipped to the drawing he'd made of the print in the shower room at school. "Look! It matches, even down to that little circle on the right print." He bent down and measured it with his hand.

Before Xena could answer she felt a drop of

rain hit her head, and then another, and then it was pouring. London weather was like that—if it wasn't raining, it either had just stopped raining or was about to start. They ran for the Underground station.

In the train car they sat close to each other so they could talk without being overheard. Luckily a group of students got on and were making enough noise to drown out most sounds.

"Did you get a good look at him?" Xander asked. Xena shook her head. "Me either." Xander sounded as disappointed as she felt.

"I'm not even sure it *was* a him," Xena said. "Whoever it was had that hood pulled up, and anyone could have been wearing jeans."

"Well, at least we know something about his shoes. Or her shoes. What was that tour guide saying, anyway?"

"That tall thing is an obelisk. You know what that means?"

Xander nodded. "Like a column, only squared off with a pointy tip, like the Washington Monument."

"Exactly. That one by the Thames is Egyptian, and it's called Cleopatra's Needle. Get it? It's a needle without an eye."

"Wow!" Xander exclaimed.

"It was in London when the amulet was stolen, and it was something that people would know about. The riddle must be from Sherlock's time and not a translation of an Egyptian saying or anything, because the Egyptians didn't call the obelisk Cleopatra's Needle."

"That means it's a clue about where the amulet is. It *must* be something that Amin wrote and left for his descendants to find!"

As soon as they got home, Xena checked out the guide's information. "Listen to this, Xan," she said breathlessly. "There's another obelisk in Paris—that's across the Channel, not across the sea. *But* there's a third obelisk in New York, and it's also called Cleopatra's Needle. That must be the 'sister across the sea'!"

"Now we're getting somewhere!" Xander said, but then his face fell. "Are we supposed to go to New York? How can we do that?"

"Let's look at the riddle again."

They went into Xander's room and pulled the fragile piece of paper out of its envelope. Xander read:

"I am a needle but cannot sew.
I have no eye and cannot see.
I face my sister across the sea,
and toward my sister you must go."

"Aha!" Xena said. "We're supposed to go *toward* the other obelisk, not all the way *to* it. And look—the writing under it says 'five hundred yards'! So we're supposed to start off at the Cleopatra's Needle in London and go five hundred yards in the direction of New York, which is west!"

Xander pulled his map out of his pocket. He figured out roughly five hundred yards due west from the Egyptian monument. The spot was in a jumble of buildings, and it was hard to tell exactly which one was meant. "Anyway," he said, "New York isn't exactly west from London. It's south too."

"But if we get a globe and draw a line between London and New York, it won't be accurate enough to tell us what's five hundred yards away!" This sounded like one of those impossible word problems in math: *If London is X miles north and Y miles east of New York, what will be the angle of the line that you draw between the two cities, relative to the equator, and what will you find five hundred yards along that line?* Xena was good at math, except for word problems. They mixed two different things—math and language—and her orderly mind had a hard time with that.

Xander smiled in the infuriating way that

meant he had figured something out ahead of her. "Be right back." He disappeared into the living room, and she heard him rummaging around in the gadget box. He came back wearing the GPS watch that their mother had said was too small to be useful.

"London. Cleopatra's Needle," Xander said into the watch. They heard a few beeps. "New York. Cleopatra's Needle." More beeps. "Connect." Then, "Five hundred yards. Enlarge. Aha!" He showed Xena the small screen where a tiny red dot blinked on the map of London. "That's the spot!"

She squinted at it. "Okay! Let's go!"

They were on their way out the door when their father appeared from the kitchen. "Whoa! Where do you two think you're going?"

"Out, Dad." Xena was impatient. "We're working on a case, and we just got an important clue about—"

"Have you finished your homework?"

Xena sighed in exasperation. "Not all of it."

Actually, she hadn't even started it.

"It's okay," Xander said. "I'll go. It's just a few Tube stops away."

"No, you won't," their father said. "Not by yourself on the Underground. Besides, it's getting late. We'll be eating dinner soon. Xena, get back to work, and, Xander, you find something to do. The case can wait until tomorrow."

No it can't! Xena wanted to say. We have less than a week left! But she knew there was no point in arguing, so she slumped down at the table.

Xander gave Karim a call. "Making any progress?" Karim asked.

"A little." Xander explained about the obelisk. "We're going back tomorrow to see what's there. And we think someone was following us." He told Karim about the hooded figure whom Xena had chased. "Can you meet us after school? We can tell you about it, and you can go with us to the place we think the clue was talking about."

"Super! I have a piano lesson on Tuesdays, but it's over in an hour."

That night both Xena and Xander had a hard time falling asleep. When Xena finally did, she had a series of strange dreams about ancient Egyptian gods. As a tall, lean human figure with the head of a long-beaked bird leaned over her, its glittering eye fixed on her, she woke with a start. She lay there, her heart pounding, while her head cleared.

It was just a dream, she told herself, but in the dark quiet of her room, anything seemed possible. Had Thoth come to visit her? And if so, was he asking Xena and Xander to help find the amulet?

Or had it been a warning?

CHAPTER EIGHT

It was still drizzling the next day, so PE was indoors. After a while Xander asked permission to go into the locker room and use the bathroom. The coach nodded, hardly paying attention to him before turning back to the boys still passing the ball to one another.

Xander felt uneasy in the locker room by himself. Usually it was crowded with talking, laughing boys. Now it was silent, and he could hear every creak and pop of the old building. Someone had left a showerhead dripping, and the rhythmic *tap-tap-tap* of the drops hitting the tile got on his nerves. He went into the shower room and turned it off.

He looked around, thinking back to last Friday when Karim first told him about the case. Where had the mysterious eavesdropper hidden? The shower stalls were separated by shallow partitions. You could see into almost all of them just by standing in the doorway, and he and Karim had gone all the way in. There was only one way out—through the locker room. Nobody had gone that way or the two boys would have noticed.

Or *was* there only one way out?

Xander looked around. Six shower stalls lined one wall. On the back wall was the janitor's utility closet. Next to it—he stopped and looked again. The closet! Someone must have been hiding there!

No, that couldn't be it. Mr. Franklin had been mopping the floor when they were in there, and he would have seen a person in the place where he kept the mop and bucket.

"'When you have excluded the impossible,'" Xander quoted his famous ancestor softly, "'whatever remains, however improbable, must be the truth.'" It was improbable that someone had hidden in the closet, but everything else was impossible.

He had to get a look into the closet somehow. He wished he'd asked the SPFD for a set of lock-picking tools. Halfheartedly he turned the knob, and to his surprise, the door opened. Silently, he noticed. Someone hiding in there could have come into the shower room, and he and Karim never would have heard a thing.

Then he noticed something else. At the back of the closet, a thin line of light ran along the floor. There was another door! Whoever had come in had done it after the janitor had removed his supplies. That was why Mr. Franklin hadn't noticed.

Where did the door lead? Xander closed his eyes and pictured the floor plan of the ground floor of the school. Aha! This was the same janitor's closet as the one near his locker. Someone must have come in through the hallway.

Now he was getting somewhere. Xander had been careful not to disturb any evidence. He went back into the locker room, feeling around in his backpack. There it was—the multipurpose tool that he always carried, with a small flashlight and magnifying glass.

Back in the shower room, he squatted near the door to the closet and ran the light over its walls and floor. He saw rags, cleaning solution, and an industrial-sized vacuum cleaner. And something else. On the floor was a dusting of what looked like spilled cleaning powder. He peered over to look at it more closely, but the powder got up his nose and he sneezed. The force of his sneeze was enough to blow the powder all over, scattering it.

But not before he saw that there were footprints in the dust. Familiar footprints, made by athletic shoes, with a little circle in the middle of the right one.

Xena couldn't concentrate in her classes. They had found out enough about each of the clues to give them some hope that they'd solve the case—but then they had hit a wall. It was so frustrating. All she could think about was finding the spot that was five hundred yards along the line between the two Cleopatra's Needles.

But what if they were wrong about the clue? And even if they had the amazing accuracy of a GPS to pinpoint exactly five hundred yards, what if in Sherlock's time the measurement had been off? Even if the measurement had been accurate when Karim's great-great-great-granduncle, Amin, wrote the clue, Xena couldn't help remembering that one hundred years had passed. Buildings were torn down and new ones were built; people threw things away; objects broke. Even if he'd left something, they had no guarantee it was still there, and if it was, how would they know when they'd found it? It would hardly have a sign on it saying CLUE!

So she wasn't paying much attention when

she heard someone calling her name as she finally made her way to her locker.

It was Hannah. "What's your problem?" She knocked gently on Xena's forehead. "Hello? Anybody home?"

Xena forced a laugh. "Sorry! I was thinking."

"Obviously! I wanted to know if you could come with us. There's no football practice today, so Shane and I are going to have tea around the corner. I think Jake's coming too."

"I can't. I have to do something with my brother."

"Oh, Xena, you're not his babysitter!" Hannah pouted. "He can do whatever it is on his own!"

"My parents don't like him to travel alone," Xena said. "He's only ten!"

"When I was ten—"

But Xena didn't find out what Hannah had done when she was ten, because at that moment Xander came up behind her.

"Ready?" he asked.

"See you tomorrow," Xena said to Hannah. Hannah didn't answer, but turned away and joined some other people who were zipping up their jackets. Xena felt herself flush with anger. Maybe Hannah wasn't such a good friend, after all, if she got so rude at a little disagreement.

Xena followed Xander down the corridor, trying not to look back at the others as they burst out laughing. She hoped it wasn't at something Hannah had said about her. "What's your hurry?" she asked her brother. "We have an hour before Karim's piano lesson is over."

He wasn't paying attention. "Another clue!" He told her about the footprint. "Someone *must* have been listening to me and Karim that day," he finished. "It's probably the same person who made the threatening phone call."

"And the same person who was following us down by the river! When he saw he couldn't scare us off the case, he must have decided to follow us," Xena said. "Time to figure out who it is. Let's find out what kind of shoe made that print."

Hannah forgotten, Xena headed to the library, where the after-school program's homework hall met. With Xander looking over her shoulder, she typed rapidly on a computer, starting a search. A few sites came up, but they were all about selling shoes, not showing what their soles looked like. She tried again, and still nothing.

"Give up," Xander said. "Not *every*thing is on the net."

Xena brightened. "I bet the SPFD knows a shoe expert. Let's see if we can find Andrew."

But Andrew had already gone. Xena tried to call him and left a voice mail when he didn't answer. She figured he must be on the Tube, where cell phones didn't work.

"I'll make a better drawing," Xander said. "We're going right to the business part of London, and there must be all sorts of places where we can send a fax." Using his memory and the sketch in his notebook, he drew a more detailed picture.

"Okay," Xena said. "Let's go, or we'll be late!"

Karim was waiting for them outside the Tube station nearest to the spot on the map.

"I'm glad you're here," he said as they came up the stairs. He shot a nervous glance over one shoulder. "I think I'm being followed."

"Followed?" Xena and Xander chorused. Someone was following Karim too?

Karim nodded and looked around again. "I keep seeing someone, but I can't get a good look at him. He keeps hiding behind things."

"Are you sure it was a him?" Xander asked.

"I think so, but I'm not sure," Karim answered.

"We've got to lose him," Xena said. "We can't risk having him figure out where we're going and get there ahead of us. Let's split up and meet right here." She pointed at the map, showing Karim the point that Xander had determined was five hundred yards past the obelisk. "Ready? Go!"

The boys took off running in different directions. Xena pretended she had to tie her shoe, hoping that whoever was following them would have been taken by surprise and wouldn't react in time to follow one of the boys. That way, if the unknown person wanted to stay with one of them, he—or she—would be forced to follow Xena. And I'll give you something worth following! she thought. The track coach had recently been training her on hurdles, and she was itching to put her new knowledge to good use.

She shot off, dodging and twisting through the streets. When she found herself camouflaged by a large crowd, she ducked into a doorway and flattened herself, panting, to see if a slim figure in a hoodie would pass. Nothing. As soon as the sidewalk was clear, she broke out of the doorway and sprinted in the opposite direction. Someone was unloading boxes from a van onto the sidewalk. Finally! Something to jump over. She cleared the first one and leaped over the second. The man unloading the boxes shouted at her, but some other people cheered. Great! That would attract the attention of the shadowy figure.

She kept running until at last she was sure she

had shaken any pursuer off her trail. Then she made her way, still taking unexpected turns and occasionally whirling around to check behind her, to where she had agreed to meet the boys.

They were standing under an awning, pretending to inspect the objects in the window. Hmm—hardware. Not likely. Good thing nobody seemed to pay attention to them. "See anyone?" Xena asked.

"No," Karim said, and Xander said, "Me either." He added, "I faxed Andrew that paper, by the way."

"What paper?" Karim asked.

"Tell you later," Xena said. "What is this place, anyway?" The building that towered at the end of the square looked like a Greek temple, with columns and steps, but above it soared a steeple.

"This is St. Martin-in-the-Fields," Karim informed them.

"What is it, some kind of museum?" Xander asked.

"No, it's a church."

A church? It hardly seemed likely that someone would hide a clue about a missing Egyptian amulet in a house of worship. Still, you never knew.

The rain started up again, and this time it

was more than a drizzle. They ran up the stairs and through the large door into the building.

They were greeted by the sound of music and people standing at their pews. A service was just starting. "We can't go in now," Xena whispered. "It's not respectful. Let's find someplace to get out of the rain and come back later."

On the porch again, they surveyed the street. They'd have to run through a large open space to get to shelter, but there appeared to be some shops around the corner.

"Let's go that way." Xena pointed to the right. "We'll stop at the first place where we can sit down and figure things out."

Fortunately they came upon a pub almost immediately. They ducked inside, water pouring off them, and hung their wet things on hooks by the door.

"Phew!" Karim said, surveying the crowd. "We're not the only ones getting out of the rain."

Xena spotted a couple getting up from a table and managed to snag three seats for them.

"So what's going on?" Karim asked.

Xena and Xander filled him in on the phone call, the strange person they'd seen lurking around the obelisk, and, most of all, the new clue about the needle.

"Wow!" Karim's eyes sparkled.

"The real question," Xena went on seriously, "is who could be after the amulet?"

The man wiping the counter swiped at their table with a damp cloth. They ordered cocoa. "What brings you kiddies out in this weather?" he asked.

"We're—um, we're looking for something," Xander said.

"It's kind of a scavenger hunt," Xena added. She thought that if they mentioned a missing Egyptian amulet, the man would think they were either crazy or making fun of him. And in a way, it *was* a scavenger hunt.

"Oho, so you need to bring something back that proves you were here?" The man seemed pleased by the idea, so Xena didn't want to contradict him. She smiled in what she hoped was a neutral way.

"Here, take one of these." He picked up a coaster from the next table and handed it to her. On it was written the name of the pub, The Cat and Crown, and below it, "R. S. Collins, proprietor."

Xander said, "Thank you, Mr. Collins."

"Oh, I'm not Mr. Collins!" He laughed. "Mr. Collins passed away years ago, poor old soul.

No, I just work here. The proprietor is his widow, Mrs. Rosie Collins. She's not here today, but the pub's been in her family for over a hundred years."

Xena wasn't paying attention. She was staring at the coaster.

A large group left, and the waiter went to clear their table. As soon as he was out of earshot, Xena said, "Look at that!" She pointed to the pub's logo.

"So what?" Xander asked. "Lots of pubs and restaurants have strange names—like The Slug and Lettuce."

"Turk's Head," offered Karim.

"The Green Man."

"The Bishop's Finger."

"The—"

"Not the name," Xena broke in. "I mean, not that the name is strange. It's the picture—it's a cat wearing a crown! Bastet is the cat goddess—and in this restaurant she's a queen. A ruler! This is where Bastet rules!"

Karim studied the coaster. "What about the rest of it—she Bastet rules?"

"I don't know," Xena admitted. "But I bet we'll find out. It's got to be the same place!"

CHAPTER NINE

"Anything else, kids?" The waiter had come back with three mugs of steaming cocoa while they were talking. Xena looked at Xander as though to say, *You're on!* The man had been friendly, but he was clearly busy, and Xander's famous charm might help if they wanted him to stay and talk for a minute.

Xander flashed a smile at the man. "My sister and I are from the States," he began.

A snort. "I could tell that!"

Xander had gotten used to people commenting on his accent. "We don't have places like this there, at least not where we live in Florida. How old is the pub?"

The waiter seemed pleased at their interest. "More than two hundred years. Been in the same location all this time."

"Wow!" Xena was genuinely impressed.

"Here, look at this." The waiter went behind

the counter and beckoned them to follow him. "Look here." Scratched in the wood were words, some numbers, and what looked like abbreviations. "These are the prices of things that they served here long ago." Xena and Xander looked for something—anything—that could be a clue. There were no hieroglyphs or anything that looked Egyptian. No drawings of the sun, either.

"Where did the name come from—The Cat and Crown?" Karim asked.

"I don't rightly know." The man rubbed his chin. "Why don't you come back tomorrow and ask Mrs. Collins? She's here most afternoons except when she goes to visit her son, like today. Will there be anything else?"

"This case is frustrating," Xander said as they fastened their raincoats. "Every time we get close to something, we hit a dead end."

"All we can do is come back, like the waiter said." Xena felt just as gloomy as her brother. They walked through the rain with Karim to the corner where his mother was going to pick him up.

"There's something I don't get," Xander said as they hurried along, heads hunched against the drizzle. "Why did Amin write down the clues? Why didn't he just tell his brother or somebody where the amulet was?"

"I bet he didn't get a chance," Xena answered. "He was in hiding. Then, after he was caught, the brothers probably didn't have a chance to talk again."

"Plus I don't think he wanted his brother to have it," Karim added. "It wasn't until he was dying that he gave up on getting it himself and sent that clue to my great-great-great-grandfather. He must have figured it was better for someone in the family to have it than for the amulet to stay hidden forever."

"Why didn't he just call?" Xander asked.

Karim shook his head. "It must have been really expensive to make a phone call from Egypt back then. He was only an archaeologist's helper and then a guard, and he probably never got either of those jobs again after what he did in London. He must have been really poor. If he wrote a letter, it would probably get intercepted by the police, so he wrote that clue instead. The police wouldn't think it had anything to do with the amulet, so they'd let it through."

"Anyway, I don't believe that Amin was making up all that stuff about the amulet." Xena was convinced of this. "He must have been angry, and he might have wanted to make Sherlock look stupid by sending him on a wild-goose chase, but Sherlock took it seriously, and he wasn't easy to fool."

They rounded the corner and saw Karim's mother waiting to pick him up. They politely refused her offer of a ride and rode home on the Tube instead, a gloomy silence between them.

After supper and homework, Xena went to find Xander in his room. "Let's try to get things in order," she suggested. "We have a lot of clues—we just need to find out some answers. Maybe there's something we missed in the casebook."

"It's in my locker at school," Xander said. "I didn't want to drag it around in my backpack in the rain. What if it got wet and the ink ran?"

"You *left* it?" Xena was astonished. "What about the school thief?"

"It's locked up! Anyway, who would want the casebook?" Xander suddenly felt uneasy about what he had done, but he didn't want to admit it. "It's not valuable to anybody but us—it's just an old leather notebook. Who would steal it? Besides, I remember everything that was on the pages where Sherlock wrote about the amulet, so we don't need it today."

This was true; with Xander's photographic memory he'd never forget something he'd read. Still, Xena knew she wouldn't be comfortable until they had their hands on the casebook again.

"You could have wrapped it in plastic or something. How could you leave it?"

"What did you want to investigate?" Xander tried to change the subject.

"I don't know. I thought if I looked at the clues, I might think of something. But I can't do that now because you left it at school. I can't believe you'd do such a thing."

"Stop worrying, Xena. You always think you know better than me. I didn't do anything wrong. It's in my locker. That's why they got us lockers, remember? To keep our stuff safe from the thief." Xander didn't convince even himself with that one, and of course Xena wouldn't let him get away with it.

"Oh, sure," she said in a tone that made him shrivel inside. "Those lockers are one hundred percent safe. They should use them in the bank!"

"The school gets locked up at night!" he shot back.

Their voices had risen, and the sound of their argument brought their father in. "Go to bed, you two. You're obviously sleep-deprived or you wouldn't be bickering like this. What's gotten into you, anyway?"

They glanced at each other and then looked away. "Nothing," Xander said sullenly. He could not admit to his father that he had put the precious casebook at risk. *It's perfectly safe,* he told himself as he brushed his teeth and washed his face.

They got to school early the next day, both gloomily aware that they had only three days left to find the amulet. Hardly anyone was there yet, and they headed straight for Xander's locker. Xena caught sight of Hannah, Shane, and Jake turning a corner ahead of them. Maybe she and Xander would find the casebook right away, and then she could go join them before class.

Xander opened his locker. He reached down to pick up the books he'd placed on top of the casebook the afternoon before.

Even before his fingers touched the first one, he knew the worst had happened. The pile was too short, and the math book he had left on top was now below his history book.

The casebook was gone!

The only reason Xena didn't say "I told you

so!" was that the look on Xander's face was so horrified she didn't want to make him burst into tears right there, in front of the people who were starting to arrive. "Pull yourself together!" she hissed at him. "Look for clues! Is there anything in your locker that you didn't put there?" She hoped the anger in her voice covered the dismay that she felt. The casebook was one of a kind and was their link to their great-great-great-grandfather. They had just started solving the cases. Would all the rest of them remain unsolved forever?

Xander pulled everything out of his locker, scattering papers, pens, and dirty gym socks all over the floor. He pawed through the pile frantically.

Nothing. Not a single indication of who could have taken the casebook. They stared at the mess in disbelief.

"The thief would have had to be really dumb to leave us his ID," Xander finally pointed out. "Maybe we should start investigating the school thief. Whoever took the casebook could be the same person who's been stealing all those other things."

"How do you know it's a him?"

It was a good point. Xander had been

assuming that, since he suspected someone had been listening to him in the *boys'* locker room, but now that they knew the person must have come in from the hallway, it could be anyone.

"Who was already at school when we came in?" Xander asked. "I saw your friends—"

"What difference does that make?" Xena snapped. Why did he automatically assume it was one of *her* friends? Still, she tried to remember. They were so early that hardly anyone was there. "It could have been someone after school yesterday or someone who got here for the before-school program or band rehearsal. Or one of the teachers!"

"Probably not a teacher." Xander felt so miserable he could hardly speak, but he forced himself to think. "It would be risky. Teachers don't hang out around the lockers. Whoever took all those things must be a kid."

"How do we know that the school thief also took the casebook?"

"We don't," Xander had to admit. "But it could be."

They stood thinking furiously as the hall filled up with more and more students. Then the bell rang and they had to go to class.

The day passed slowly. At lunch Xena picked

at the peanut butter sandwich her mother had made her. It was her favorite, but she just couldn't eat. A tray slid onto the table next to her and she looked up. It was Andrew. "Something wrong?" he asked as he cut up the piece of mystery meat that was generally served as school lunch, and which was the reason that Xena and Xander usually brought their own.

She shrugged. She couldn't admit to Andrew, of all people, that the notebook was missing. It had taken them a long time to make friends, and she knew how easily he lost his temper. This time she couldn't blame him, so all she said was, "Case isn't going well."

"I don't have any word yet on the hieroglyphs, but I do have something that might help." He handed her an envelope. Xena recognized the return address: it was from the SPFD.

"Did they already find someone who knows about shoes?"

Andrew nodded, his mouth full. "Read it," he said around the mystery meat.

Xena quickly scanned it. "They got it!" For a moment she felt her heart lift, but then it fell again. "Oh. The shoes are Atalantas."

"What's the problem with that?"

"Too many people wear them. I don't know

how we'll narrow it down." Ever since most of the track medalists in the last Olympics had worn Atalantas, they'd become the most popular brand of sports shoes in the world.

Xena read the rest of the report. Men's shoes, British size 9, equivalent to American 9½. The shoe expert hadn't been able to figure out what the circle in the print could be.

So now they had to look at the soles of people's shoes. But how could they do that? And even if they did find the eavesdropper, that wouldn't prove that it was the same person who had taken the casebook. And it wouldn't get them any closer to the amulet.

She slid the paper back in the envelope and tucked it carefully in her notebook. "Thanks," she said to Andrew.

"Glad to help. Oh, no—look who's coming." It was Hannah, closely followed by Shane.

"What's the matter with them?"

"Don't like them. She's a snob, and he's a pain."

Jake trailed Shane into the cafeteria. "Jake's not so bad," Xena said.

"He's not vile, like Shane," Andrew agreed. "But he's moody."

"What do you mean?" Xena asked.

Andrew shrugged. "I don't know. I guess he's decent enough, just distracted or something." Andrew shoveled the rest of the grayish meat into his mouth, followed it up with a long gulp of juice, and stood up. "I'll let you know if I hear anything else from the SPFD. See you later."

The rest of the day dragged. Xena and Xander didn't even have the prospect of going back to The Cat and Crown to look forward to, since Xena had to study for a test and their parents wouldn't let Xander travel around the city on his own. Karim would be tied up at a piano recital.

So Xena's mood was no better when she stood next to Xander as he dug around in his locker to get out everything he would need that evening.

"Hurry *up,*" she said again. The corridor was deserted; everyone had either gone home or to homework hall.

"Why don't you just go without me?"

"Oh, sure. Dad would kill me if I left you." But it was tempting.

At last Xander wrestled his backpack out of the locker. He knew it was crazy, but he couldn't help leaning in and checking just once more for the casebook. Something prickly moved up his arm. “What in the world—?” He dropped his pack and pulled up his sleeve.

Clinging to his arm, its little claws straight up and its wicked-looking tail curved high in the air, was a pale brown scorpion.

CHAPTER TEN

For an instant Xena crazily thought that the scorpion must be the amulet, because she could have sworn that time stood still. Then time unstuck and she ripped a poster off the wall and used it to knock the creature off Xander's arm. She leaped forward and upended a trash can over the scorpion, trapping it.

She grabbed Xander, forgetting for the moment about the casebook and the amulet, thinking only of her brother and the danger he'd been in. "Did it sting you?" Xander was trembling but managed to shake his head. She released her bear hug and stepped back, still keeping hold of his shoulders. "Are you sure?"

"What's going on here?" It was Dr. Holloway, the science teacher.

Xena explained about Xander finding a scorpion in his locker.

"I'm going to call your parents," the teacher

said, his face grim. "Where did it go?" Xena pointed at the upside-down trash can. "Good thinking," the teacher said approvingly. He slid the poster under the trash can, and then carried the whole thing into the science room.

By the time their mother arrived, Dr. Holloway had deposited the furious-looking scorpion (along with rolled-up papers, tissues, and candy wrappers) into the terrarium. "I'm so sorry, Mrs. Holmes," he kept saying. "I can't think how it could have happened. I know the scorpion couldn't have escaped on its own." He showed her the latch, which was securely closed.

Their mother nodded. "I see. No, I agree that it couldn't have escaped without help. Has anything else been interfered with?"

Dr. Holloway swept his eyes around the classroom. "Nothing that I can see right now. Xander assures me he wasn't stung, but if you want to run him by the hospital—"

"No," Xander said. "Please, Mom." He pulled his sleeve up and his mother inspected it for what felt like the hundredth time.

"A scorpion sting isn't deadly," Dr. Holloway went on, "but it's very unpleasant. I understand that in Mexico one name for a scorpion is 'three bee stings,' because that's what it feels like."

"There's no need for the hospital," Mrs. Holmes said. "It was clearly a prank—not a very nice one, but a prank nonetheless."

The teacher promised to call the principal and launch an investigation the next day, and their mother took them home.

Their father was waiting for them in the kitchen. He gave Xander a hug. "I hear you had a close call. You okay, son?"

"I'm fine." Xander was becoming uncomfortable at all the attention.

"Didn't you get a harassing phone call the other evening?"

Xena and Xander assured their parents that nothing was wrong, that they'd tell them if there was a problem, that school was fine, all the while backing out of the kitchen and into the living room, leaving their parents talking to each other.

"Okay, this is getting serious." Xena's voice was grim. "Someone is after the amulet. They stole our casebook, they made threatening calls, they put a scorpion in your backpack—"

"And don't forget, someone's following us around. It's possible that these things aren't being done by the same person, but it would be a really weird coincidence if they weren't. Let's try to narrow it down, okay? I bet whoever was in the locker room is someone on the soccer team. That way, if he was caught in school late, he would just say he was practicing."

"Or someone who hangs around the soccer team a lot." Xena couldn't help thinking of Hannah.

Before Xander could answer, the fax machine whirred and spewed out a piece of paper. She leaped on it. "It's from Andrew!"

"Finally!" Xander joined her at the fax machine and ran his eyes down the page. "It's about the hieroglyphs, from someone named Dr. Bowen. He says the writing is gibberish. What's that? I thought it was Egyptian!"

"'Gibberish' means 'nonsense,'" Xena explained. "Great. Another clue that leads nowhere."

Xander was still reading. "Dr. Bowen says that the Egyptian symbols don't make any words, just letters. Look, he wrote them out here." He pointed to the row of hieroglyphs with letters underneath them: *f-t-h-r-n-g-l,* then a space, then *s-m-y-t-h*.

"Well, *that's* a big help." Xena was discouraged. "We have to go back to The Cat and Crown. There *must* be something there. We went five hundred yards along the line and found a pub that was there in Sherlock and Amin's time and that shows a cat like Bastet as a ruler. It can't be a coincidence."

"Let's go now," Xander said, but Xena shook her head.

"It's too late. All that scorpion talk took a lot of time. Let's work ahead on our homework, okay? And then tomorrow we'll ask Mom if we can go out for an hour or so after school. Why don't you call Karim later and see if he can go?"

"I want to look for the casebook," Xander said stubbornly.

"Whoever took it must have something to do with the amulet, right? So if we solve the amulet problem, we'll also find out who took the casebook."

"Maybe not. Maybe it was the school thief who stole the casebook."

Xena threw her hands up. "Come *on*, Xander. The school thief takes only expensive things that are small and easy to hide, like a watch, Jill's MP3 player—"

"That graphing calculator," Xander added.

"Right, and the necklace that girl left in her desk, and money. It's *possible* that the same person took the casebook, but not likely. It's too large. It couldn't be hidden in a pocket."

Xander nodded. "Either the thief took the casebook after everyone went home so that he wouldn't be seen lugging it down the hall, or it's still there, in someone's locker."

"Too bad we can't stake out the lockers all day." Xena's voice showed her frustration, which she was trying to hide. "Let's assume it was someone who was at school after hours."

"In that case, it's most likely the same person who was listening to me and Karim."

"Right! Like I said, if we solve the amulet problem, we'll also find the casebook thief."

Xander sighed heavily, and Xena took pity on him. She put her hand on his shoulder. "We'll find it. I just know we'll find it."

But Xander wasn't comforted. He reached for his backpack. "I have a math quiz on Friday. I'll study for it now, so I won't have to tomorrow and we can go out."

Friday! Was the day after tomorrow really Friday? No way would they be able to find the amulet by Saturday. It felt as if they hadn't made any progress at all.

He opened his math book, and a piece of paper fell out. Even before he picked it up, Xander knew he hadn't left it in there. He felt impatient. Was Karim playing his silly note game again? He unfolded the paper. Instead of another cryptic story about Dr. Watson and Sherlock Holmes, he saw a crude drawing of a scorpion. Scrawled below the sketch were the words, *Keep away from the amulet or you'll never see your casebook again!*

CHAPTER ELEVEN

The next day Karim was out of school, but he texted Xander to say that he was at the dentist and would meet them at The Cat and Crown after school. Sure enough, when they entered the pub, they saw him waving to them from a table. The weather was a little better, and the place was even livelier than it had been two days earlier. Some people were playing darts, others were eating big sandwiches, and still others seemed to be celebrating a birthday.

"Did you order something?" Xena asked as she slid into the seat next to Karim's.

He shook his head. "I was waiting for you." He was smiling, his eyes shining. "I saw my granddad yesterday. I told him that you were on the case and we were making progress. He was so happy! He says that when he comes home from the hospital he wants you to visit so that he can thank you in person. That's the first time he's talked about coming home!" Xena and Xander didn't react. "What is it?" Karim asked.

"We had some trouble." Xander looked over at his sister. He couldn't bear to talk about the casebook.

Xena swallowed. There was no easy way to tell this. "Someone stole our casebook."

Karim looked from her to Xander and back again, his brown eyes wide open in astonishment. "*Stole* it?"

Xander nodded. "And left a scorpion in my backpack."

"Did it sting you?"

Xander shook his head.

"Still," Karim said, "it could have, and it would have been all my fault."

"No, Karim—" Xander protested, but the other boy went on.

"Yes, it would. This is getting too dangerous. We have to stop. What if—"

"What about your grandfather?" Xena interrupted. Karim fell silent.

"We're being careful," Xander said. "Really. And a scorpion isn't deadly. Besides, I don't want this jerk, whoever he is, to think he can scare us off the case."

Xena nodded. "And we're making some progress."

Xander handed him the note with the drawing of the scorpion on it. Karim read it and looked up. "I don't get it. How is this progress?"

"It proves," Xena said, "that whoever took the casebook is the same person who left the scorpion. It also proves that they know about the amulet. We already figured that, but it's good to have solid evidence. So now we know that anything we learn about either case will help us with the other one. Did you ever mention the amulet to anyone except us?"

"Never." Karim sounded definite.

"Not even a hint?" Xander asked.

"I promised my granddad that I wouldn't say anything to anyone except you, and I wouldn't even do that until I figured out that you really were good detectives and hadn't just found that painting by accident."

"Okay, then." Xena settled back in her seat. "So once we find the person who was spying on you two in the locker room—"

"And who keeps following us around and made that phone call and left the scorpion and the note in my backpack—" Xander added.

"We'll have the thief *and* the casebook."

"It must be a student," Xander said. "Probably a boy. The person Xena saw was dressed like someone our age and was too short to be an adult. And more boys than girls wear Atalantas."

"Now we have to find Mrs. Collins," Karim said.

"Let's play the Game!" Xena said.

"What game?" Karim looked mystified.

Xander explained that their father had taught them to play a game that had been passed down from Sherlock Holmes, where they had to guess something about a person just by looking at him. "Like you can tell someone's a teacher if he's carrying schoolbooks," he said. "Maybe we can figure out who Mrs. Collins is."

There were a lot of women in the pub, some old, some young, some with friends, a few with one other person, and two sitting alone. Both Xena and Xander thought hard; each wanted to be the first to find her.

The waiter said her husband died years ago, Xander remembered. She must be old. Or at least not young.

She owns the pub, Xena thought. She would know all the regulars.

A cheer came up from the people playing

darts as a short woman threw her arms in the air in triumph. A bright-eyed elderly woman sitting at a table near them was laughing as she congratulated the short woman on her darts victory. "I always told you you'd win someday, Selma!" she said, and the short woman bent over to give her a quick hug and a kiss on the cheek. As she did so, a small face poked up from the elderly lady's lap. A cat—like Bastet!

"Mrs. Collins!" Xena and Xander said at once. The lady looked around at them and smiled.

"Who talks to her?" Xander asked in a low voice.

"You, of course." Xena was confident in her brother's ability to charm anyone, particularly an old lady who seemed as nice as this one.

They all got up and went to her table. The woman looked up at them and smiled as she stroked the sleek black cat sitting on her lap.

"Are you Mrs. Collins?" Xander asked.

"That's right, dear. Rosie Collins, proprietor. And who might you be?"

"I'm Xander Holmes. This is my sister, Xena, and our friend Karim Farag." Xander took a deep breath. It all sounded so crazy, but he did his best. "We're searching for something, and we think we're supposed to find it here."

"What kind of something, dear?"

"That's the problem," Xena said. "We're not sure." She stroked the cat, which arched its back under her hand and purred more loudly. Xander sneezed and backed up a step, rubbing his nose.

"Well, then, I can't really help you, dear."

They racked their brains trying to think. How much could they tell Mrs. Collins without giving away the whole story of the amulet?

"Your cat is beautiful," Xena said.

"Thank you, dear. The women in my family have always kept cats, because of the name of our pub."

Xander nudged Karim, who looked bewildered. "'Who Bastet rules, she Bastet rules'—it means 'The person who runs The Cat and Crown rules Bastet'!" he whispered.

"As much as anyone can rule a cat!" Karim whispered back.

"The name of our pub and the Egyptian connection, of course," Mrs. Collins went on, "what with my name and all."

Her *name*? Rosie Collins? That didn't sound Egyptian! "I don't understand about your name, Mrs. Collins," Xena said.

"Rosetta Stone Collins," the old lady answered proudly. "My family has always had an interest in everything Egyptian, you see. It started with my great-grandparents, who had a friend from Egypt."

"Rosetta Stone—like that famous stone in the British Museum?" Xena asked. "The one that helped people figure out how to read hieroglyphs?"

She chuckled. "Yes, just like that. My great-grandmother thought Rosetta was a pretty name and it went well with our last name, so she asked my mother to name me Rosetta Stone in remembrance of her dear friend. Then I married Mr. Collins and became plain Rosie Collins!"

"What's the Rosetta Stone?" Xander asked.

"I saw it at the British Museum," Xena said. "Remember, Xander? Mom made us go to all those museums before we started school."

Xander shook his head. "You must have gone to see it when I was looking at the mummies."

Karim said, "It's this big stone that has writing on it in Egyptian hieroglyphs and some other languages. . . ." He hesitated and looked at Mrs. Collins.

"Greek and demotic." Mrs. Collins took up the explanation. "A great French scholar named Champollion could read Greek, and he used it to decipher the Egyptian."

"Wow!" Xander said. "Another clue!"

"A clue to what, dear?"

Xena and Xander looked at Karim. "I guess it's all right," he said. "Go ahead and tell her." He dropped his voice to a whisper. "But not about the magic."

They explained that they were descendants of Sherlock Holmes working on a case. When Xena said the name "Amin," Mrs. Collins sat up straight. The cat jumped off her lap and stalked away, looking offended.

"Amin Farag—that's the friend of my great-grandparents!" She turned to Karim with a look of astonishment. "Did your friend say your name is Farag?" Karim nodded. "Are you related to Mr. Amin Farag? Did you come to find the paper he left?"

More paper. I hope this one actually leads us somewhere, Xena thought, and she said, "Yes, ma'am. Do you have it?"

"Isn't that strange! All these years and nobody shows any interest in it, and then yesterday a boy came here and was interested in it, and now you! How odd that the three of you would turn up right after him."

"What boy?" Xena asked.

"Just a boy. About your age, I'd say. Brown

hair. I didn't get a good look—it was dark yesterday, you know, and the lights in here are dim." Brown hair—that could be a lot of people.

"What did he want?" Karim asked.

"He said that his father collected Egyptian artifacts and had heard a rumor that I had something Egyptian. I told him no, nothing like that, unless he meant the paper Mr. Farag gave my ancestors for safekeeping until he or his son could come back for it."

"Oh, no!" Xander exclaimed. "You didn't give it to him, did you?"

"Of course not!" All three of them felt huge relief, only to be followed by worry when she added, "I did show it to him, though. He seemed most interested in it, examining it under the lamp over there. He wanted to take it outside, but something about him didn't seem trustworthy, so I told him he couldn't and asked Harold over there"—she nodded at the waiter, who was bringing them the tea and lemonade they had ordered—"to keep an eye on him."

"Mrs. Collins," Karim said. "Amin Farag was my great-great-great-granduncle. I don't think he had any children. I'm the closest thing to a direct descendant there is." He pulled his school ID out of his pocket and showed it to her.

Mrs. Collins glanced at it with her bright eyes, and then seemed to make up her mind. "You three wait here," she instructed. She disappeared into a back room while they burned with excitement.

Mrs. Collins returned with an envelope. On it was written in spidery, old-fashioned handwriting, *For Mr. Amin Farag or his son. To be called for.*

"It was among my great-grandmother's possessions at her death. My grandfather didn't know what to do with it. It has remained in the family for all those years."

She passed it ceremoniously to Karim, who made a little bow as he took it from her hand. After a deep breath, he opened it. Xena and Xander stared eagerly at him, but the disappointment Karim felt showed in his eyes as he passed it to them.

Nothing but a series of meaningless doodles on both sides.

"What does it mean?" Xena asked.

"Sorry, love, I've no idea. All I know is that it was to be kept for Mr. Farag, and now I've done my duty, even if a century late." Mrs. Collins nodded at Karim, who managed a weak smile. "And now I've got to get back to running the pub. Your snacks are on the house!"

They thanked her and went out into the darkening afternoon. "I wonder why you have to hold it to the sun," Xander said.

Xena shrugged. It didn't matter; the sun was barely showing.

"That must be why that other boy held it to the light in the pub," Karim said.

"Good thing the lights aren't too bright in there!" Xena said.

"How do you know they weren't bright enough to see whatever it was he was supposed to see?"

"Because," Xena explained, "if he'd gotten what he needed, he wouldn't have tried to take it away!"

"Maybe there's a watermark," Xander guessed. "You know, when paper looks like there's nothing on it but there are some marks that show in the light. Like on English money."

"American money too, sometimes," Xena said. "Let's go someplace brighter."

Karim glanced at his watch. "I have to go home," he said. "Walk me to the Tube? My mum said I could ride alone just this once."

They went down the stairs with Karim. "It's pretty bright down here," Xander said, and Karim held the paper up to the light.

"Nothing." He passed it to them and they checked it out. He was right.

"Can I borrow it?" Xena asked. "We'll take it by the SPFD and see if someone there can find something. Whatever it was must have faded."

Karim handed her the envelope just as his train came in. Xena and Xander waved good-bye and were turning to go when Xena, who was looking at the map, said, "Look, Xander—we're not far from the British Museum. Let's go look at that stone on our way. Maybe there's something like these marks on it!"

"But I want to figure out who that other person was—the one who got to the pub ahead of us!" Xander protested.

"We can't split up. You can't take the Tube alone, and I think it's more important to figure out the clue. We don't have anything to go on with that other person—just that it's a boy with brown hair. That could be lots of people!"

They cut through the park in Russell Square, dodging pigeons as they went, and entered the British Museum. The Rosetta Stone stood in its case right near the entrance. It was a large, dark gray slab covered with tiny writing in three different languages. Not one of them looked anything like the marks on their paper.

Once again they had to step aside when a tour group came by. The guide told the tourists about the stone and how it had been used to decipher hieroglyphs. "The first complete English translation of the Egyptian portion of the text was made in 1858, but today most people prefer the later work of Fotheringale and Smythe, two young scholars at Oxford, whose translation is considered more poetic, even though it departs somewhat from the original. . . ."

Xander yawned but then he caught sight of Xena, who had a broad grin on her face.

"What is it?" he asked.

"I know what the hieroglyphs from the casebook mean!"

CHAPTER TWELVE

You know what the hieroglyphs mean?" Xander couldn't help sounding doubtful.

"Yes!"

"Tell me about it on the way to the SPFD. It's getting late!"

They hurried out of the museum and ran down the steps. "It'll be quicker on foot," Xander said, so they trotted down the sidewalk, dodging pedestrians.

"Okay, so it turns out that hieroglyphs don't use many vowels, not the same way that our alphabet does," Xena began.

"How do you know?"

"Read it. What were those letters that Dr. Bowen said the hieroglyphs stood for?"

"F-t-h-r-n-g-l, then a space, then s-m-y-t-h."

Xena nodded. "That's what I thought. Didn't you hear what the guide said?"

Xander stopped dead in his tracks.

"Fotheringale and Smythe—the people who translated the Rosetta Stone. That's what the hieroglyphs spell!"

"So put it all together. Amin wanted someone—his son or his grandson—to read the Rosetta Stone. Of course they wouldn't know how to read hieroglyphs, so he had to send them to a translation—the Fotheringale and Smythe version!"

They soon found themselves in the neighborhood they had lived in when they'd first arrived in London. They hurried to the headquarters of the SPFD in a secret room at the back of the Dancing Men pub. They had discovered the door to the headquarters as part of a test that the SPFD had given them to see if they had inherited Sherlock Holmes's powers of deduction. First they had to go through the main room of the pub and down a long corridor to a storage room. Inside the storeroom a large box, which looked as if it were made of cardboard, was pushed against a wall. The box was really made of concrete—and it concealed the small door. Xander crawled inside the box and set the dials on the actual door to the combination he had figured out: 221B, Sherlock Holmes's street address on Baker Street.

Xander pushed the door open and crawled through. As his feet disappeared, Xena took a deep breath and followed him. She always hated this part. She didn't like small, enclosed spaces, and even the breakthrough about the Rosetta Stone didn't distract her enough to make her comfortable.

Andrew met them as they emerged into the club's sitting room. "So what's the excitement?" he asked as he helped them to their feet.

Xander gave him a quick rundown of the case, leaving out the part about the amulet's supposed power to make time stand still.

"Interesting!" Andrew raised one eyebrow. "Let's have a look at Sherlock's notes." An uncomfortable silence filled the small room. "What, don't have the casebook on you? Bring it by school tomorrow, then."

Xena looked at Xander, who looked down at his shoes. "I can't," he finally said. "It's disappeared."

If Andrew had yelled at them, it would have been better than the stony silence followed by his bitter exclamation, "I knew it! I *told* Aunt Mary you weren't to be trusted."

"But—"

"But nothing. You're too young to be given

such a treasure. You don't even care about it or about Sherlock Holmes! Just wait till the others hear about this." Andrew stomped off and slammed the door behind him.

"Do you think he'll tell everyone?" Xander asked.

"Probably." Xena couldn't bear the thought. "Let's leave the paper from Mrs. Collins with a note asking someone to send it to that Egyptologist."

"If we leave the real thing, it might get lost like the casebook," Xander objected, "and then Andrew will get us kicked out of the Society."

"He won't. We'll find it first. Besides, the others wouldn't let him do that to the descendants of Sherlock Holmes." Xena wasn't as sure as she sounded. "Give it to me and I'll make a copy."

She headed into the office, where Mr. Brown, the Society's secretary, was clicking on his keyboard. He looked up and smiled at them. "Xena! Xander, my boy! How are you two?"

"Fine," Xena mumbled, hoping he wouldn't mention the casebook. "Can I make a copy?"

Mr. Brown waved his hand at the photocopy machine. "Be my guest!"

She placed the paper facedown on the glass.

She'd have to make a copy of each side, but the marks were faint and didn't show up well on the first try. She pressed a few buttons and tried again. Better, but still not great. She increased the contrast to the maximum. This time it came out so grainy that it was almost worse. She was about to drop that attempt into the recycling bin when Xander grabbed her wrist.

"What?" she asked, twisting free.

"Look!" He pointed at the paper.

"I don't see what— Oh!"

The light from the copy machine had been so bright, and the contrast had been increased so much, that the marks from the front were overlaid on the marks from the back.

"They're numbers!" Xander said. "Two, eighteen, thirty-five, ninety-one, forty-four."

Their eyes met. "The Rosetta Stone!" Xander breathed. "It's *got* to have something to do with the translation!"

Mr. Brown cheerily interrupted his work to give them directions to the nearest public library. "Thanks!" they called out as they dashed away, and for once Xena didn't notice how closed in she felt crawling out through the box in the pub's storeroom.

• • •

In the library Xander went in search of the book—the Fotheringale and Smythe translation of the Rosetta Stone—while Xena called their mother to tell her they were close to home and would be there soon. "Yes, Mom, we're all caught up on homework," she was saying when Xander reappeared waving a piece of paper with a call number on it. She gestured at him to go find the book while she finished talking to their mother.

"Phew!" Xena settled next to Xander, who was turning the pages of a large book in a dark gray binding. "Mom wants us home soon. Maybe we should check the book out."

"Can't." Xander shook his head. "Reference only. See?"

Someone had written things in the margins of some of the pages. Was that what they were looking for? They checked pages two, eighteen, thirty-five, ninety-one, forty-four, but some of those pages had nothing handwritten on them and others had notes that didn't make much sense. "C-f-r Budge? What on earth is that?" Xander wondered out loud at one of them.

"I don't know," Xena said, "but if it means nothing to us, it probably wouldn't mean anything to Amin's descendants either. It's got to be something that makes sense. Let's start at the beginning of the translation, not in all this introduction stuff."

Xander turned pages until he came to the actual translation. He read, "The timekeeper," and stopped. He turned sparkling eyes on Xena. "Timekeeper!"

"Go on," she said.

> The timekeeper tells of the prince who has followed his father as king, ruler with sparkling crowns, greatest, who rules the land of Egypt and worships its gods, stronger than his enemies, who brings safety to its people, lord of the Festival of Thirty Years, like the great god Ptah, like the sun-god Ra, who rules both Upper and Lower Egypt, son of the Philopatores gods beloved by Ptah, granted supremacy by Ra, like unto Amun the son of Ra, King Ptolemy the eternal, also beloved by Ptah, in year Nine of his reign. . . .

Xander counted silently and found the second, eighteenth, and all the other letters: *h-s-s-w-h*. No help there.

But in the meantime, Xena was counting the words and scribbling down what she came up with: *timekeeper, greatest, safety, year,* and *thirty*.

"Look, Xander." She pointed at it.

"That doesn't make much sense."

"It makes more sense than 'hsswh'! And remember, it talks about a timekeeper. That can't be a coincidence!"

"You're right," he conceded. They thought for a moment.

"Who's the greatest timekeeper?" Xena asked. "Thoth, god of time?"

Xander shook his head. "If this is a key to where the amulet's been hidden, then it's not a who. It's a *what*. A safe place—"

"Wait a second. Let's think like Sherlock. Examine the evidence, not what we think we're looking for. The amulet's first hiding place, the water clock, was a timekeeper, so the greatest timekeeper could be a bigger clock. 'Greatest' can mean 'biggest' too, not just 'best.'"

"I know!" Xander jumped up. "Big Ben!" The clock in the tall tower at Westminster Palace was once the biggest clock in the world and was still one of the most famous.

"Big Ben's the bell, not the clock," Xena reminded him.

"Duh! But you know what I mean. The clock in the tower where the bell is."

"All right. But what about 'year' and 'thirty'? Maybe Karim's grandfather was wrong and the amulet works once every thirty years instead of every fifty!"

"Why would Amin say that in code? Anyone who was looking for the amulet would already know how it worked and wouldn't care if it was every thirty years or every fifty. I think this is telling someone where to find it, not what it is."

"Wait!" Xena counted again. "What if 'sun-god' is one word instead of two? Then we get 'nine' instead of 'year.' Big Ben at nine-thirty?"

Their eyes met over the pages of the book. At last they were getting somewhere!

CHAPTER THIRTEEN

They still didn't know exactly what they were looking for. They were pretty sure that they had to go to Big Ben and do something at 9:30, but what? And 9:30 in the morning or night?

I hope it's 9:30 in the morning, Xander thought. There's no way Mom and Dad would let us go there so late. Just as he thought that, Xena's cell phone rang. *Oh, please let it not be Mom and Dad!* Xander thought as hard as he could, but it was no use.

"Hi, Mom." Xena rolled her eyes at him as she spoke. "Yes, I know. But it's not that late! And we have a case that—but, Mom—but—" She frowned and kicked the ground while their mother's voice came through the phone. "Okay. Be right back."

"Let me guess," Xander said. "Dinner, homework, it's getting dark—right?"

Xena nodded. "You left out 'You two should know better!'"

"Maybe Sherlock Holmes didn't have a computer and GPS," Xander said as they headed for the flat. "But at least he didn't have a *curfew*!"

Xena managed to get most of her homework out of the way before dinner and went online to investigate a trip to Big Ben. She found the nearest Tube stop and then tried to find out what hours the big clock-tower was open. Her "Oh, *no*!" made Xander look up.

"What?" he asked, and his heart sank as he saw her face.

"We can't get in." She pointed at the screen. "You can only go up inside the tower if your MP gets permission for you."

"What's an MP?"

"Member of Parliament, like your member of Congress. Only we're not British, so we don't even *have* an MP."

Xander read the text on the Web site. "What makes it worse," he said, "is that people *used* to be able to get inside. That means that Amin could have gone in there and left something. It has to be something inside. If it was outside, people would have noticed it by now."

They sat in discouraged silence for a moment, and then something occurred to Xena.

She turned to the keyboard and typed rapidly for a moment.

"What?" Xander asked.

Xena shook her head. "I'll tell you if I get an answer." She turned back to finish her homework, and checked her e-mail every few minutes. After her fourth attempt, she said, "Aha!" and turned the screen so that Xander could read the message.

It was from Mr. Grayson, the curator at the Timekeepers Museum. "You two really are clock buffs, aren't you? As it happens, I have some research to do at Big Ben and can easily get you in. I'll move my appointment up to tomorrow and see you there after school."

"Yes!" Xander pumped his fist in the air. But Xena looked disappointed. "What?" he asked.

"After school is nowhere *near* nine-thirty," she pointed out.

Xander's face fell but then he perked up. "We can at least get a look around," he said. "We might find a way to go back there at nine-thirty. It's better than nothing."

The instant school was out on Friday afternoon, Xena and Xander met up in the corridor. People were slamming lockers all around them, but

Xena still lowered her voice. "Do you have your Tube map?"

Xander nodded and pulled it out with difficulty, as a soccer ball took up most of the room in his backpack. "Here's the nearest stop to Big Ben." He put his finger next to a drawing of a tall steeple with a clock on it.

They squeezed through the crowd and raced to the Tube stop. The ride seemed to take forever, but finally they got to the stop right by the Palace of Westminster.

The huge, rectangular tower loomed over them as they hurried toward the palace. It was beautiful—four clocks with white faces under a pointy spire, at one end of the majestic palace. Pale clouds floated behind it, making it look as if the tower were gliding slowly across the sky.

"Wasn't Big Ben bombed during World War Two?" Xena asked Xander as they neared the stone building.

"Uh-huh. Two of the clockfaces were damaged." Neither one said what they both were thinking: *What if whatever we're looking for was destroyed?*

They saw Mr. Grayson waving to them from the base of the tower. They broke into a trot and arrived next to him.

"I'll sign in and then we can go up," he said. "All right?"

"Great!" Xena and Xander chorused, and watched as he went to talk to a man in a uniform.

Xander saw two familiar figures approaching. He nudged Xena and pointed out Jake and Shane, who were walking together and talking to each other. "What are *they* doing here?" he asked.

"Coincidence?" Xena hazarded, but she knew that wasn't likely. London was a huge city, and it wasn't like these native Londoners were there to see the sights.

She felt uneasy and moved closer to Xander, who muttered, "Something's up." She nodded in agreement.

"What are you doing here?" Xander asked as soon as they were within earshot. The boys looked up, surprise on both their faces. Was it his imagination, or was Shane's surprise fake?

"What are *we* doing here? What are *you* doing here?" Shane asked.

Xena said, "We're going up the bell tower!"

Xander groaned. Why did she have to tell them?

"Good for you!" Jake said. "How did you manage that?"

Xena explained without mentioning the amulet. But all the time she was talking, something was nagging at her—an odd sound. She couldn't figure out what it was, only that it had come from one of the boys. "Why don't you ask if you can come up with us?" she suggested.

Jake and Shane looked at each other and shrugged, and then Jake said, "Why not? Might be fun."

As the boys walked off together down the paved path, Xander turned to her, furious. "Are you nuts?" he demanded. "Why did you invite—"

"Hush!"

"What?" Xander was surprised. His sister sounded excited.

"Listen!" she hissed.

He listened. Nothing but some birds, some of the ever-present tourists, a baby crying.

"Can't you hear it? That clicking sound!" Xena whispered. "There's something on the sole of Shane's shoe!"

Xander thought for a moment. How could he find out what he needed to know? Then a grin broke across his face and he pulled the soccer ball out of his backpack. He stood on the wide sidewalk, kicking it in the air, trying to keep it from touching the ground.

When the older boys came back with the news that they'd gotten permission to go up the tower with them, Xander was still kicking it around. At first the two older boys didn't pay any attention to him—they stood talking with Xena—but as Xander purposely kept flubbing an easy move, Jake finally took pity on him. He said, "Let's go over there and I'll show you how to do it." He pointed to a small park across the street where a statue of the famous British prime minister Winston Churchill seemed to glower at passersby. Xander picked up the soccer ball and followed him, trailed by a bored-looking Shane and a curious Xena.

"Here, kick it to me," Jake said, and Xander complied. They passed the ball back and forth a few times, and then Xander copied what the older boy had shown him. Shane joined them, and they kicked the ball to one another.

"Bet you can't steal it from me!" Xander said when the ball came in his direction. He took off, dribbling it past Shane, who couldn't resist the taunt. Xander shot a meaningful look at Xena, who moved closer just as Xander pretended to lose his footing. He stuck a foot in between Shane's ankles and tripped him up.

As Shane went sprawling, Xena ran up.

"Here, let me help you." She gave Shane a hand. "Xander, you're such a klutz!" She beamed triumphantly at Xander. So she'd seen something!

"I couldn't help it," Xander whined. "It's slippery. Did I hurt you, Shane?"

"*You* hurt *me*? Hardly." Shane brushed mud off his knees. "I'm used to spills."

Xander was dying to ask Xena what she'd seen, but at that moment he saw Mr. Grayson standing at the base of the clock tower, gesturing at them. They all grabbed their backpacks and ran to the tower.

"Now keep close to me," Mr. Grayson warned as one of the guards unlocked a door. "I've told them that you're serious students of timepieces and won't behave like silly kids."

He led them up the winding stairs, Xena at his heels. Xander wanted to catch up with her and find out what she'd seen, but Jake and Shane were in between them, and the stairway was too narrow for him to pass. He wondered how Xena was feeling in there. Was the narrow space making her uncomfortable? Or was it okay, seeing as there were small windows every once in a while that allowed a glimpse of the world outside?

The walls were stone, and although they looked slimy, they were dry. They were cold and rough, though, and the stairs were worn where countless feet had stepped on them. The banister was black metal and felt even colder than the walls.

They climbed and climbed, turning always to the right as they made their way up the seemingly endless spiral staircase. Mr. Grayson had to stop a few times and catch his breath, and each time, Xander tried to slip past the older boys. "Here, who are you shoving?" Jake asked.

"I just wanted to walk with Xena," Xander protested.

"Grow up," Shane said. "Big sis is walking with us."

Xena wished she could drop back and join Xander, but even if she did, she couldn't say anything to him without the others hearing. It was such a narrow place, and the cold stone walls echoed the smallest sound. People had scratched their names into the soot-darkened walls, which somehow made it even creepier. The windows that let in a little pale light were few and far between, and the higher they went, the tighter Xena's chest felt.

Finally they arrived at a landing that was a bit wider than the others, where the stairs changed direction. They paused and Xena took a deep breath, fighting the panicky feeling.

Xander managed to squeeze past Shane and Jake. He passed Xena too, as though his one goal were to get to the head of the line, and as he did so, he leaned in so close that his curls tickled her face and she was able to whisper directly into his ear, "Tack in shoe!"

So that was what made the clicking sound, and more important, it explained the circle in the shoeprint. It took all of Xander's willpower not to confront Shane then and there, but he knew that this still wasn't proof of anything. The prints he'd seen had disappeared, and he had no evidence that they'd ever existed. And even if people believed him that Shane had been in the janitor's closet and in the shower room at school, that didn't mean he had taken anything or even that he had put the scorpion in Xander's backpack. Probably a handwriting expert could prove Shane had left the threatening note and maybe someone could even trace the phone call Xena had received, but all that would take time.

And time was something they didn't have. He didn't even have the time to feel angry at the danger the other boy had put him in.

"Can you look at the clockworks from in here?" Xander asked Mr. Grayson.

"Yes, that's how they repair them. They even have to go in and clean things once in a while."

"Brilliant!" said Jake. "Just wait until I tell everyone that I got to go inside the works at Big Ben!"

"No, it's much too dangerous," the man said sternly. "I'm not even allowed in there without an official. I'm just here to look at the documents a caretaker wrote during the First World War. You four will have to stay quiet while I do that, and then we'll all go down together."

"Did the caretakers write that too?" Xander pointed at the graffiti that was all around them.

"Some," Mr. Grayson said. "But until recently visitors could come in here whenever they wanted, and I'm afraid that people can't resist leaving their mark. Some of the marks have historical interest. See, up there is the signature of the actress Laura Sears, and below it . . ."

He went on, showing them the names of people they'd never heard of, but Xena and Xander weren't paying attention.

Incised into the stone was something familiar—the outline of a hand with an eye drawn in the palm.

CHAPTER FOURTEEN

Xena and Xander tried desperately not to stare at the familiar symbol. If Shane hadn't noticed the carving, they didn't want to draw his attention to it. Xander glanced at it out of the corner of his eye. It had obviously been there for a long time. Dust and soot had gathered in the lines, making the symbol nearly invisible except when the light came in at a slant, as it was now doing. The late afternoon light made the shadows deeper and the contrast with the wall around them sharper.

Mr. Grayson paused to catch his breath. Xena cast about for something to ask him that would make the boys pay attention to her and not look around. What could you ask about a clock?

"Um, I guess the clocks are so old that they aren't very accurate."

Sure enough, the man perked right up.

"Some of these old timepieces were astonishingly accurate. Much more so than many watches your parents and I used to wear! But it *is* big," he conceded, "and sometimes something would get into the mechanism or a piece would wear out from heavy use. In the old days, they would put a penny on the minute hand to slow it down if it was going too fast, but of course now we have better ways of regulating it. Did you know that there is a prison cell in the tower?"

"For thieves?" Xena couldn't resist glancing at Shane.

"No, actually for misbehaving MPs!" Mr. Grayson said with a chuckle. "The cell hasn't been used in quite a while. The chimes are famous."

Shane's attention seemed to be all on their guide at this point, so Xander risked another glance at the hand, knowing that what he saw would be instantly imprinted on his brain. Above the hand, almost hidden by the soot deposited by early-twentieth-century London, was the carving of a crude clockface. It had no numerals, but its hands were clearly pointing to 9:30! So the clue about 9:30 had nothing to do with the time they should visit the tower. It meant that they should look for a clockface indicating that time.

And in the instant before he looked away again, Xander saw something that made his heart skip a beat. The hour hand wasn't a simple line. It was an arrow.

The carving was far out of Xander's reach, but he knew that his sister, with her rock-climbing skills, would have no trouble reaching the arrow. But how to tell Xena about it without alerting Shane?

Mr. Grayson turned to head up the stairs again. Xander was desperate. He brushed against Shane, pretended to stumble, and yelled, "Ow! Cut that out!"

Xena whipped around to face him. She could tell that Xander was faking. But why? His eyes were telegraphing something to her, but she didn't understand.

"What's the problem?" Mr. Grayson came down a few steps.

"They shoved me," Xander whined. "They tried to push me down the stairs!"

"Did not!" Jake was indignant.

"Did too!"

"You're a liar," Shane said hotly. "*You* pushed *me*!"

"You're a clumsy oaf," Xander said, and sniffled.

Xena put an arm around him, bending down to his level. "Did they hurt you?"

He leaned against her as though he couldn't put any weight on his right foot, and managed to breathe into her ear, "Clock above hand—hour hand—is an *arrow*," before Mr. Grayson reached him.

Xander saw understanding flash across Xena's face as she straightened. She nodded slightly.

"Enough," the man said. "Can you walk?"

"I think so," Xander said.

"All right, then." He sounded disgusted. "Down we go. All of us. I'll have to come back another day."

Xena bent to tie her shoelace. "Be right with you," she called as Mr. Grayson herded the three boys, Xander limping dramatically, in front of him.

As soon as they rounded the bend, she leaped for the wall. She knew she had only a few seconds, but luckily the pitted and scarred stone gave her plenty of finger- and toeholds. In a flash, she was running her hand along the line indicated by the arrow.

Nothing.

She shifted her weight a little farther and reached out even more.

"What's keeping you?" came from below.

"Knot in my shoelace!" she called. "Got it now! I'm coming!" And at that moment, her fingertips reached into a rough hole.

Heavy footsteps were approaching from below. Mr. Grayson must be coming back. She dug her fingers furiously into the hole, and the tip of one finger touched it.

It was a thin piece of something. It felt hard and cold, like metal.

CHAPTER FIFTEEN

Xena had barely grabbed the object and dropped back down when Mr. Grayson's head poked around the corner of the winding staircase. "What's taking you so long?" He sounded furious. Poor guy; it had been hard for him to climb the stairs and now it was all wasted. Xena promised herself that once they found the amulet, they would explain and try to find some way to make it up to him.

"Sorry." She squeezed past him and hurried down the stairs. She didn't want to leave Xander with Shane, even if Jake was there too. Mr. Grayson's footsteps grew fainter behind her as he made his careful way down.

Outside, Xena spotted her brother hanging out near a group of people who were pointing up at the tower and consulting a guidebook. Good—he'd had the sense to stick close to adults. Shane wouldn't dare do anything in front of them.

Shane, his hands on his hips, was scowling at Xander, while Jake stood a little apart looking uncomfortable. Xena ran up to them and stood next to her brother.

"So what was *that* all about?" Shane's voice was a snarl, and Xena flinched.

"You know what it was about," Xander shot back. "You've been following us and making prank calls to our house. And what about that scorpion?"

"That—" Shane shook his head. "You're daft," he said coldly.

"Oh, come off it," Xena said. "We know it was you."

"You know what was me?" Shane's voice rose until the tourists, who had moved away, turned and stared.

Jake put his hand on his friend's arm. "Come on," he said. "Let's go. He's playing some kind of game with us. See you Monday, Xena." He tried to tug Shane along with him, but Xander stepped forward.

"Oh, yeah?" Xander challenged Shane. "Then how do you explain the tack in your shoe?"

"The tack in my shoe?" Shane looked bewildered. "What are you talking about?"

"Come *on*, Shane." Jake sounded anxious, and Xena narrowed her eyes and looked at him.

"Go on," Xander said. "Let me see the sole of your shoe."

With the air of humoring a crazy kid, Shane held Jake's shoulder for balance and kicked his left foot up.

"Not that one," Xander said. "The right one."

Shane heaved an exaggerated sigh, rolled his eyes, and lifted his foot. "See? Nothing." But Xander darted forward and scraped at the area near the toe with his fingernails. A clod of mud fell off, revealing the bright shine of a tack head.

"All right, so there's a tack in it." Shane sounded a little abashed to be proven wrong. "I don't know how Jake got it and I don't see—"

"How *Jake* got it?" Xena looked at the other boy in confusion.

"Yes, these are Jake's shoes. He loaned them to me because I forgot to bring my regular shoes to football practice. We went to Jake's house before we came here and he gave me these. He wanted to come look at Big Ben for some reason." Shane snorted. "Now are you satisfied?"

But Xena and Xander weren't paying him any attention. They were staring at Jake, who had turned red. "It was you?" Xena asked softly.

Jake nodded, not looking at her. He shrugged Shane's hand off his shoulder and stood with his hands dug deep into his pockets, his eyes on the ground. "You might as well go home, Shane," he said. "I'll see you Monday, okay?"

"But—" Shane began, then he shrugged. "Okay. See you." He walked away, casting one look back at them.

Xena, Xander, and Jake stood in silence. The tour group had drifted away, leaving them alone. The buzz of traffic and the gurgle of pigeons was all they heard.

Xena couldn't stand it anymore. "Why, Jake? Why did you do those things?"

"It's my mum." He kicked at a small pebble and then stopped.

"What about her?" Xena asked.

"You remember how I told you she works at the university?" Xena nodded. "Well, she teaches archaeology. They've been trimming the budget at the university, and it looks like she's going to be made redundant."

"Huh?" Xander was bewildered.

"Laid off," Xena informed him. "Like fired, only not because of anything that's her fault."

"Right." Jake nodded. "She loves her job, and she's been sad ever since she found out. Anyway, last Friday I forgot my gear in the gym, so I took a shortcut through the janitor's closet. I had just stepped in when I heard that boy—Karim?" Xander nodded. "I heard Karim say something about a missing ancient Egyptian amulet. If my mum found something like that, I'm sure they'd keep her."

"Is that what you were looking for?" Xander asked cautiously. He didn't know how to bring up the magic. "Just a regular old Egyptian amulet?"

Jake looked as though he might smile if he weren't so miserable. "I don't know what's so regular about an ancient Egyptian amulet. Was there something special about this one?"

"No," Xena said. "Not that we know of." It wasn't really a lie; she still didn't know how she felt about the whole time-standing-still business.

"I'm really sorry," Jake said. "I didn't know that scorpion stings hurt so much until Dr. Holloway made his announcement about it. I thought it would just scare you."

Xena and Xander knew they should be angry, but Jake looked so miserable that they couldn't.

"How did you find out about The Cat and Crown?" Xena asked.

"I followed you. Your friend, actually. I listened to you talking to the waiter, and the next day I went back and met the old lady. Then today I was following you again. I couldn't get rid of Shane, but he didn't notice you." He wouldn't, Xander thought. "I heard you mention Big Ben in school, so I figured that was where you were going. And there's something else." Jake reached into his backpack and pulled out the casebook.

Xander whooped and grabbed it, then clasped it to his chest. "I'll never let it out of my sight again." He closed his eyes to let the relief sink in. "How did you get into my locker?"

"Shane showed me how one day." Jake looked, if anything, more ashamed. "We were bored, and he knows how to open any kind of lock."

Xena and Xander each knew what the other was thinking—as soon as this was over, they were going to investigate the school thefts, even if they had nothing to do with Sherlock Holmes. It probably wouldn't take much to prove that Shane was the culprit.

"I read that note you left in the casebook," Jake went on, "you know, the one about holding the secret to the sun?" They nodded. "But the lady in the pub wouldn't let me take the piece of paper with me. I didn't know what to do after that. That's why it was such a piece of luck overhearing you at school talking about Big Ben."

"You have to tell Dr. Holloway that it was you with the scorpion," Xena said.

"Oh, I will," Jake said fervently. "I want to get everything off my chest."

Xander glanced at his watch. "Xena, it's getting late! Tomorrow is when the fifty years are up. We still have some investigating to do. I'll call Andrew and tell him we're on our way." He started walking away while punching in a number on his phone.

Xena looked at Jake, who was standing with his hands in his pockets, staring down at the ground. She felt like saying something to him but didn't know what. She finally settled on, "See you Monday," and he nodded without looking at her. She turned and followed Xander, pulling from her pocket the object she had found in the bell tower. It was dull gray metal, and scratched on it were two rows of hieroglyphs.

She caught up with her brother. "Tell Andrew we're going to need to see Dr. Bowen again, the Egyptologist." Xander relayed that information, then folded up his phone. He took a firmer grip of the casebook as they started off in the direction of the SPFD. Xena turned back just before they rounded a corner and saw Jake still standing where they had left him, looking very small against the immense building, and very much alone.

"We have the casebook! We got it back!" they shouted as they squirmed through the tiny door into the Society's meeting room. A crowd of people—Aunt Mary, Mr. Brown, and four or five others—stood waiting for them.

"Congratulations!" Mr. Brown beamed at them. "I knew you'd find it!"

"You're lucky you did," Andrew said, but he looked relieved, and not as grumpy as his words sounded. "Dr. Bowen, the Egyptologist I consulted before about the hieroglyphs, is on her way. Come have some tea while we wait."

When Dr. Bowen arrived, Xena gasped and nudged Xander.

"What?" he whispered.

"Don't you recognize her?" Xander shook his head. "It's Jake's mother!"

Dr. Bowen bent over the piece of metal that Xena had placed on the table. The Egyptologist sighed, shook her head, and straightened up. "Whoever wrote this wasn't a scholar, I'm afraid, so it's hard to tell exactly what they intended to say. The top line does look like an attempt to write something in Egyptian, but the second line is nonsense, like the first sample you sent me. It appears that the person who wrote this consulted Sir Alan Gardiner's *Egyptian Grammar*—no, that wasn't published until 1927, and you told me this is earlier than that, correct? Perhaps he had access to—"

"Thank you," Andrew interrupted. "But we don't really care at the moment which book he used. Can you tell us what it says?"

Dr. Bowen leaned over the piece of metal again. "Well, it's quite rough, and as I said, the grammar is execrable." Finally she said, "More or less—and mind you, this is just the best I can do and the meaning might be somewhat different, but more or less the significance is, 'That which you seek is in the hand of the pharaoh.' "

" 'The hand of the pharaoh?' " Xena echoed. "But there aren't pharaohs anymore, and I don't think there were any in Sherlock's time either."

"I know!" Xander burst out. "A mummy!" But which one? There were hundreds of mummies all over! The British Museum alone had lots of them.

"Which symbols mean that?" Xena asked, and Dr. Bowen moved over to show her the top row of hieroglyphs.

"But what about those other letters?"

"They're not really letters," Dr. Bowen started to explain. "Egyptian hieroglyphs aren't an alphabet, but a syllabary—"

"But do they *spell* anything?" Xander asked.

"Not a thing."

"What letters—or syllables or whatever—do they stand for?" Xena asked.

Glancing at the hieroglyphs, Dr. Bowen wrote *K-R-B-R-R-Y-M-S-M*.

"The Carberry Museum!" Xena and Xander sang out together.

CHAPTER SIXTEEN

Xena glanced at her watch. The museum must be closed by now. "But we can't wait until tomorrow!" She felt close to tears. "It might be too late! We have to get to it now!"

"Too late for what?" Dr. Bowen asked. They launched into an explanation, leaving out the part about Jake's involvement. It was up to him to tell his mother, not them.

"The Thoth Clock!" Dr. Bowen's eyes widened as she reached for her cell phone. "I've heard about that. And there was an amulet hidden in it?" She punched some numbers into her phone. "I don't know about the part about time standing still, but it does sound to me as though there's reason to make some inquiries. Hello, Nigel? Excuse the ring at home, but I have something rather urgent." She filled him in on the story. "Yes, yes, I know it sounds odd, but I can vouch for the Society. Yes, I see. I'll ask." She covered the mouthpiece with her hand. "Just what is it you need to know?"

"Are all the mummies in display cases or are any out in the open?" Xander asked.

"All in cases, with security," she said after consulting with the person on the other end.

"What about when the water clock was stolen?"

It took longer to get an answer to this one, but Dr. Bowen finally said, "One mummy had been purchased along with the clock and was out in the open."

"Don't you remember?" Xander asked Xena. "Sherlock said it was—" He broke off. "No, that was Karim! That day in the locker room, he told me that one of the mummies had been moved, like someone was looking for something under it, but nothing was stolen."

"Why didn't you tell me?"

"Forgot. It didn't seem important. Anyway—"

Dr. Bowen interrupted. "The mummy's hand appeared damaged at the time but they were afraid of harming it even more, so it was never repaired." She snapped the phone shut. Xena and Xander stared at her in dismay, and she smiled at their expressions. "No, we're not giving up. We're meeting the curator of

Egyptian antiquities at the Carberry Museum tomorrow."

"Why not tonight?" Xena asked.

"It will take them some time. The mummy is quite fragile. They have to call in experts and remove it to the museum's lab, which is climate-controlled, and take some other precautions as well. I'll drop you at home. Get a good night's sleep, and I'll ring you when they're getting close."

The call didn't come until late Saturday afternoon. Xena and Xander's parents drove them to the Carberry Museum. There, a guard ushered the Holmes family through the old house where Greek vases were crammed into cases, silver coins on black cloth gleamed on tables, a huge stone bull's head loomed over a doorway, and a set of what looked like ancient armor stood in a corner, its sword raised and its narrow eye slits seeming to conceal a threatening face. In a room filled with Egyptian statues, wall paintings, and the mummy of a cat, one long glass case lay empty, with a sign on it reading REMOVED FOR RESTORATION.

The guard unlocked a door marked PRIVATE and gestured at them to enter. Karim and his parents were already sitting in a sort of waiting room, along with an elderly man in a wheelchair.

"This is my grandfather," Karim said.

As Xander shook hands with him, he saw that Karim bore a strong resemblance to his grandfather.

The old man's handshake was firm. "Thank you, children," he said. "I'm glad I lived to see this day."

"You'll see many more!" Karim's father said. The adults chatted while Xena and Xander told Karim everything that had happened since they went to Big Ben.

"It was Jake all along?" Karim asked. "But he's so nice!"

"I know." Xena was still trying to get over her disappointment about Jake's involvement. "I was sure it was Shane."

They waited for what seemed like hours. Occasionally a sound came from behind a door marked LABORATORY, and once Dr. Bowen came out to tell them that they were making progress. She was wearing a surgeon's mask and a hat like a shower cap, and explained that it was important to keep modern germs from contaminating the mummy.

More time passed. They heard visitors inside the museum talking about the exhibits and exclaiming over the empty case. Someone brought them sandwiches and tea, and Xena leafed through a stack of magazines. Karim challenged Xander to a game of noughts-and-crosses, which turned out to be tic-tac-toe.

"I don't understand why Amin wrote that last message in real hieroglyphs," Karim said. "In all the other ones, he used them to stand for English letters."

"That was the most important message," Xena said. "He had to be sure that whoever read it was someone who was really serious about finding the amulet and not just someone visiting Big Ben who stumbled on the writing."

It was late when the door to the lab finally opened and Jake's mother beckoned them to come in, handing them surgeon's masks and head covers as they entered. They crowded around the table where a shriveled brownish body lay, somehow looking both pathetic and regal.

A man whose name tag read DR. ASANO was delicately picking up the fingers of the mummy's right hand with a small metal tool and putting them into a white box. "They were broken some time in the modern era," he said as a younger man scribbled down what he was saying. "Replaced quite cleverly, but you can see the evidence here"—he pointed with a gleaming instrument—"and here." The younger man put down his paper and snapped some photographs.

All the people in the room appeared to hold their breath as Dr. Asano straightened up, revealing the mummy's hand. In the palm lay a beautifully carved figurine of an ibis-headed man. Its eyes were of red stone that glittered coldly, and its kilt was inlaid with stripes of turquoise.

"Oh!" Xena breathed. "It's the amulet!"

"I think you're right." Dr. Bowen's voice was almost reverent. "It's Thoth, carved in the right style, the right material. A lovely thing." She reached in to touch it and then withdrew. "May I?" she asked Dr. Asano.

"Of course," he said. "Without you we never would have found it."

"It wasn't me." She put her hand behind her back, as though the temptation was almost too strong for her. "It was these two." She nodded at Xena and Xander.

"We wouldn't have known about it without Karim," Xander said.

"Well, somebody take the credit and pick it up!" Mrs. Holmes said. "I'm dying to see it better."

Karim's father said, "Go ahead, son. I'm sorry I didn't believe you."

"Yes," his grandfather added, "you hold it, Karim."

Karim picked up the amulet gently. For a moment he wrapped his fingers around it and closed his eyes. Xena could see that his hand was trembling.

"Let me take a picture," the young man said, and Karim opened both his hand and his eyes. While the photographer asked him to hold it first this way, then that, Karim looked at Xena and Xander.

"Didn't work," he said.

"What?" The young man took another picture. "Of course it did. I'm not using a flash, is all. It could damage the old gentleman here." He nodded at the mummy and took another picture.

But Xena and Xander knew that Karim wasn't referring to the flash.

"Can I hold it?" Xena asked. Karim passed it over. She closed her eyes and thought fiercely, *Stop, time! Stop now!*

Nothing. She had never really believed in the magic, but she couldn't help being disappointed.

Then it was Xander's turn. After a moment he shook his head and passed it back. Was the story of the magic amulet just that—a story? Had Sherlock Holmes been right when he called it "poppycock"?

Xena glanced at her watch. It was only six in the afternoon. "What time is it in Egypt?" she asked Jake's mother.

"Two hours later than London."

Eight o'clock, then. Still Saturday! So what was the problem?

Then Xander smacked his forehead. He beckoned to Karim and Xena, and they went back out into the waiting room while the adults continued admiring the amulet. "Of course the ancient Egyptians didn't mean 'midnight to midnight' when they said 'one day,' " he explained. "They meant sunup to sundown. The sun must have set in Egypt hours ago!"

They all let the truth of this sink in.

"Or maybe that thing about time standing still never was true to begin with," Xena finally said.

"Maybe it was," Karim said.

"I don't know," Xander said. "But I do know one thing!" The other two looked at him. "I know exactly where I'll be fifty years from today!"

"Me too!" Karim said.

"No question," Xena agreed. "We'll be right here! In the Carberry Museum!"

DISCARD